"You're the new agent?"

Emir's words were heavy with disbelief. "You're the one Adam recommended?"

"Yes," Kate said. "I'm K.J...."

"This won't work."

"By this, you mean me?" She took a step forward. Now she was in his face.

"That's what you meant, wasn't it? I'm not a man so..." She left the remainder of the sentence hanging.

"You need to get on the first flight home," he said through clenched teeth.

"Give me a chance."

"It's not me that's the problem."

"I know," she interrupted. "It's the customs, the tribes outside the city, the..."

"It won't work."

"Look, I know what I'm getting into. I'm qualified. I specialized in Middle Eastern studies—an exchange student. I'll help you find your sister. You just need to trust me."

SHEIK'S RULE

RYSHIA KENNIE

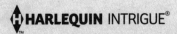

HARLEQUIN INTRIGUE®

For Rourke, who was dedicated to the art of fun.
The "Wookie Man" would have loved to rip this book to shreds,
while enjoying every word and every moment of it.

ISBN-13: 978-1-335-72093-1

Recycling programs
for this product may
not exist in your area.

Sheik's Rule

For questions and comments about the quality of this book,
please contact us at CustomerService@Harlequin.com.

Printed in U.S.A.

www.Harlequin.com

Ryshia Kennie has received a writing award from the City of Regina, Saskatchewan, and was also a semifinalist in the Kindle Book Awards. She finds that there's never a lack of places to set an edge-of-the-seat suspense, as prairie winters find her dreaming of warmer places for heart-stopping stories. They are places where deadly villains threaten intrepid heroes and heroines who battle for their right to live or even to love. For more, visit ryshiakennie.com.

Books by Ryshia Kennie

Harlequin Intrigue

Desert Justice

Sheik's Rule

Suspect Witness

CAST OF CHARACTERS

Sheik Emir Al-Nassar—Head of Nassar Security. After his parents' death, he raised his sister. Now she's been kidnapped. He must control his outrage, keep his brothers from storming the desert and bring his sister home.

K.J. (Kate) Gelinsky—Outstanding profiling skills, linguistics and knowledge of Moroccan culture make this agent the best choice to find the sheikka. But K.J.'s secret may stand in the way.

Sheik Zafir Al-Nassar—Emir's identical twin. He steps in as they race to save their sister.

Sheik Talib Al-Nassar—He must contain his rage to back up his brothers.

Sheik Faisal Al-Nassar—He heads their Wyoming branch, and can only wait and hope his brothers succeed.

Sheikka Tahriha Al-Nassar (Tara)—She keeps her brothers in line and family traditions alive. Now she doesn't know if she'll live to see her next birthday.

Adam Whitman—Second in command at Nassar's Wyoming branch. He's gone against what Emir wants, and now there's doubt that he can be trusted.

Simohamed Khain (Ed)—He was a trusted employee but has been out of touch since leaving their employ.

Dell Perrin—Moroccan ex-military.

Atrar Tashfin—He'll stop at nothing for money.

Ahmed Dahan—One of Tara's security team. Will his secrets die with him?

Baz Salem—He's in love with Tara but he doesn't stand a chance.

Yuften M'Hidi—Could hold the key to Tara's whereabouts, or he may only be a decoy.

Saffiya M'Hidi—Yuften's wife may know more than she at first let on.

Chapter One

Marrakech, Morocco
Monday, September 14, 5:54 a.m.

The first haunting notes of the call to prayer seemed troubled, almost off-key, when usually the melodious sound wove through the predawn stillness, beckoning with an easy allure not unlike the nimble fingers of the weavers in the casbah who wove the many rugs sold to the tourists. Like the rugs, the ancient chant was as much part of the rhythm of life and the fabric of Marrakech as was the still night-shrouded skyline. But today, in a mansion hidden in the depths of palatial grounds and secured by the most current technology and the best in security guards, the simple power of the timeless notes not only felt off, they were lost in the guttural roar that sounded more wounded beast than man.

Emir Al-Nassar crushed the pen in his right hand. On the desk, the smartphone lay where he had thrown it, the blue protective cover fractured, the crack running through the Blue Jays' baseball emblem. A thin line of ink ran down his arm and dripped onto the thick Persian carpet. Like blood, he thought, and wondered how much more blood would be spilled before she was safe once again.

"I won't lose her, too," he muttered thickly, his voice choked. The emotion that had welled up only seconds earlier had taken everything he had. "None of us will."

But, despite his words, the unthinkable had happened. His sister had been kidnapped.

He couldn't fathom how frightened she might be. And at this particular moment there was nothing he could do. He was at the whim of the demands of others. But inaction was not in him, no matter what they had ordered.

His mind was already jumping through a series of options. Most importantly, what action would not increase the danger that already threatened Tara and what would ultimately bring her home where she belonged. He needed to think logically, think that it was someone else's sister, that it was not Tara. It was the only way he could give everything to her rescue without the emotion he knew would only cloud his judgment.

He dropped the broken pen, not caring about the stain that might ruin the ancient carpet. He took a step away from the desk as the last notes of the call to prayer died away. He turned slowly, as if facing an executioner. Through the open blinds, the city lights shone a warm glow across Marrakech's still-shadowed beauty. It was a view he never got tired of. But today he could have been anywhere in the world for he saw none of it.

A door slammed somewhere in the hallway and suddenly the room was full of unleashed testosterone as two of his brothers, Talib and Zafir, entered the room.

"Emir, what's going on?" Talib began. "Your Jays are done and the Yankees don't play for another hour, even with the time difference, so—"

"Shut up about bloody baseball, Talib," Zafir interrupted as he looked at Emir and the silent awareness that had always run between the twins jumped like a living coil across the space that separated them. "No one cares about your fave team or even Emir's for that matter. He wouldn't call us here, at this hour of the morning, unless—" He broke off, looking to Emir for confirmation, his eyes troubled, as if expecting the worst.

"Tara's been kidnapped," Emir said with no emotion. His back was to them and he was still facing the window that allowed a view of the grounds his sister loved so much. He turned to face his brothers, schooling his features, reining in his thoughts. It was difficult, for he couldn't believe how foolish his sister had been.

"Kidnapped," Zafir repeated, a frown slicing his handsome face, his jaw clenched, his eyes blazing.

"Impossible!" Talib said as his fist smacked the palm of his hand and disbelief laced through the word. "We have one of the best security teams in the country. How?"

The word reverberated for a second, then two, as Talib and Zafir processed what this meant, how the impossible had become possible.

"She was on a night out with the girls. But, at the end of the night, she left her girlfriends behind and, it appears, her security, too. Fortunately her team caught up with her. The reports say she was with her security team just outside the gates. The evidence is in the signs of a scuffle and the fact that they left one of them dead." Emir said the words reluctantly, as if it had been his fault. "I can't imagine how they got so close to the compound—how they got her—unless security was distracted. They were two of our best." It wasn't an excuse and he still couldn't believe it had happened.

Zafir clenched his fist, his jaw tight. "She's alive?" And while it sounded like a question, they all knew it was really a command or, more accurately, a demand that she was alive or there would be hell to pay.

"As far as I know," Emir said, his voice devoid of emotion. He glared at Zafir for flirting with the reality he hadn't dared consider—that Tara was hurt, or worse. "She was taken just outside the grounds."

"She dodged her security?" Talib repeated as if not believing the possibility. "She knew the risks. She..." His voice broke and he turned away.

"When we find her, she'll be grounded for the rest of her life," Zafir snarled as if anger at her would somehow ensure his sister's safety.

"She's twenty years old," Emir reminded him. The words came almost by rote, meaningless considering the scope of what had happened. But sometimes it was difficult to remember that his sister was officially an adult. He thought of her as his little sister in need of protection. And the fact that, physically, her petite size made her almost doll-like only accentuated those thoughts. But Tara's personality was another story. It was as forward and brash as her physical being was delicate. Emir prayed that her larger-than-life personality and piercing intelligence that could challenge and often match him in many a game of chess would see her through.

"Her security tracked her, apparently found her immediately before the kidnapping," Emir continued. "The kidnappers used knives. Ahmed lived..." he said, referring to one of the men assigned to Tara. He took a breath, as if that would put reason into the insanity they faced. "He's in rough shape. It's touch and go right now. He's not able to give any information but when he is..."

"I'm on it." Zafir's jaw clenched as he said it and at the same time Talib's open palm slammed against

a vase that, at best guess, had been created over three
centuries ago. The vase crashed to the floor and none
of the brothers bothered to look as pieces flew across
the room. Instead they stood poised like predatory
animals, unmoving, contemplating the unfathomable.

Normally, Emir would have been all over Talib
and his well-known temper for breaking the vase.
He was the one who cared about the irreplaceable
items that foretold a long and venerable heritage.
But now, in a crappy and equally frightening situation, he knew Talib's anger was more than justified.

He'd felt the helpless rage himself and, as much
as he hated the emotions that had rolled through him
in the minutes since he'd learned the incomprehen-
sible truth, he couldn't stop them. He'd been at the
kidnappers' mercy. And, without consultation with
his siblings, he'd given in to their first demand in the
hope of buying time and knowing what they asked
was small enough to assure a second request, possibly even a third. That's what he told himself. The
truth was that he wasn't sure what to expect or even
what to do in this situation. The only thing he wanted
to do was to kill the men who held his sister, if he
only knew where or who they were. Kidnapping was
neither his nor his brothers' expertise.

"We'll need guns and—"

"No," Emir growled as he cut Talib off. He turned
to Zafir. "I need you to take my phone. Not now," he

said as Zafir held out his hand. "Later. That's how they'll contact us." Their voices were similar and, as identical twins, one could easily imitate the other. "When I get an idea of where they might have gone, I'm going after her—alone, at least without the two of you. All of us moving in a pack would alert the perps to what we're doing. Therefore, we all can't go. Someone—" he looked pointedly at Zafir "—has to be available for their demands. Let them believe we're waiting, getting funds together—playing the game as they want."

"There's already been a request," Zafir said quietly as he put a hand on Emir's shoulder. It was not a question; as twins there were things each had always known about the other.

"It was small. There'll be more," Emir confirmed.

Although he was by no means a kidnapping expert, he knew the pattern with other kidnappings of strangers, people he had not known or loved—people who were not his sister. And, while they weren't following the M.O. of an average kidnapper—sadly there was such a thing—he suspected they weren't unique. He moved away, slipping from his twin's abbreviated touch.

Zafir nodded. "And you've paid it."

"You think that will get Tara back?" Anger was tight in Talib's voice. He was a gifted member of their team but, of all of them, Talib had the least control over his emotions, especially now.

As always, his twin was on the same wavelength, he knew that as he saw the look of approval in Zafir's eyes. He was the one who would most likely hold his emotions in check and who could make it look like Emir was doing exactly what the kidnappers wanted—waiting and complying.

"No. They'll want more. But for now we look cooperative, and that's good for Tara," Zafir said.

"Hopefully we'll have bought enough time to get some help," Emir said.

Talib paced, his fists clenched and his jaw set. "We can't do nothing," he growled.

"Agreed." Emir paused, considering the options. He met Zafir's eyes. Although Zafir was younger by only minutes, there was never dissention because of birth order; they were usually in agreement. The slight tilt of Zafir's head told him they were in agreement in this situation, as well. His gaze went to Talib—of the three of them, the one most likely to act impulsively, more likely to insist, as he already had, that they go at the kidnappers en masse with guns blazing. He didn't blame him. They all felt the pain, the shock and the anger. For it was their baby sister they were talking about.

"For now, we act like nothing has happened," Emir said.

"No." Talib's fist clenched and he brought it down on the desk, making a trio of pens jump. His eyes met Emir's, passion blazing as his jaw clenched. His shoulder-length hair did not hide the strength in his jaw or the anger in his flashing brown eyes. "I'll kill…"

"We'll kill…" Zafir corrected. "When the time comes. First we get Tara home in the safest way possible. Too many of us would be an obvious and threatening action to the kidnappers, which will only endanger Tara. And that's one thing we will not do."

For it was not just them, Emir knew. There was their youngest brother, Faisal, whom he had yet to contact. He feared that Faisal would be on the first plane from Jackson, Wyoming, to Marrakech as soon as he heard. It was why he'd contacted their second-in-command at their Wyoming branch first, for Emir hadn't thought of a way to forestall his brother once he was aware of the situation. "Faisal…" he began as if his thoughts and his voice were one.

"I'll speak to Faisal." Zafir cut him off. "There's no need for him here. Not yet."

Emir nodded. He worried that it might take both of them to keep Faisal in the States and not jumping on the first plane. He hoped Faisal's common sense would do the job when he heard what was in place to ensure Tara's safe return.

"I spoke to Adam," Emir admitted. It was one of the first things he'd done when he'd received that devastating call just before 4:00 a.m.

Adam Whitman had been a good friend from his college days at Wyoming State and was now second-in-command in the Wyoming branch of their security agency. He was one of the few people outside the family Emir could trust. They had always had each other's back, even though, through the years, there'd been long lapses where neither one had contacted the other.

"And?" Zafir prodded.

"Adam's concerned that our family is high-profile, too well known. If this is a straight kidnapping case, that's one thing, but if there's some sort of revenge on the family…" He paused, collecting his thoughts.

"Revenge?" Talib's fist clenched and Zafir looked worried.

"We don't know, but fresh eyes… Adam might have something. The agent he's assigned will be looking at it from a different angle, without any preconceived ideas."

"He might see something we'll miss because of familiarity," Talib said.

"Exactly," Emir agreed and Zafir nodded.

"The other thing…the man he's recommending is an amazing profiler. Exactly what we need and the first thing I mentioned when I called Adam. We want nothing less than the best." He looked at his brothers, saw the pained expression on both their faces and, still, determination radiated from them. They wouldn't be beaten. He felt hope just being surrounded by them and he knew he in turn gave them hope. That was the way it had always been.

"Who is it?" Talib asked. "There've been a number of new hires in the Wyoming branch."

Emir shrugged. He'd get the name when he gave Adam the update after his brothers left. For now, names were irrelevant; he trusted Adam's judgment. "He's new, but Adam claims he's good."

Silence seemed to steep like an uneasy brew through the room as every instinct urged them to surge forward, armed-dangerous, potentially lethal as they plowed over the threat. But they were hobbled by a threat that had intelligence they weren't privy to; it knew exactly where they were and, worse, it held what they claimed most precious.

"We have no idea where they've taken her," Emir said. "Only that they want money and their demands, I suspect, will continue to go up."

Emir's stomach clenched and he ached to see his sister's kidnappers' blood seeping into the depths of the endless desert sand. But he needed something more than revenge. He needed his baby sister safe. He looked at the ink staining the ancient rug and the cracked phone, both evidence that he had lost control.

"Here's what we will do…" He motioned his brothers to sit and he laid out what had and would be done in the hours that followed.

"I don't like it, but it makes sense," Talib said ten minutes later.

"Forty-eight hours, Emir. No more," Zafir interrupted as he clapped his hand on Emir's shoulder.

"Or less if we're needed," Talib said.

"Or if you lose contact," Zafir said.

"Agreed. But if there's progress, that may change." Emir had explained his conditions and knew it was a shaky agreement. With their sister's life in jeopardy, he was surprised his brothers had agreed to that much. But they knew how delicate a situation like this was. No one had to be reminded of what they stood to lose.

Tara, the only girl in the family, with none of the brothers in a steady relationship, was all that was soft and feminine in the family. Without her, Emir knew that the niceties in life would disappear as easily as that beautiful vase beneath Talib's fist. She organized family celebrations and get-togethers, remembered family traditions. Only last month she'd gotten them all together on Skype for a toast to his and Zafir's birthday. Without her... He wouldn't think of it, couldn't.

Twenty minutes later, as his brothers exited the room, he picked up the phone. Fortunately its case was the only thing that had cracked in his initial rage. He punched the number of the Wyoming branch of their security agency. Adam picked up on the second ring.

Emir laid out what had transpired since they'd last spoken.

"Don't do anything more until K.J. gets there. Promise me." Adam's voice held an edge of concern.

Eight hours. It was a long time—it was forever. "I don't know if I can do it," he said.

"I don't know what more to say, Emir. K.J.'s already en route."

Emir sucked in a relieved breath at that.

"As we agreed, I'm sending the best. And despite the fact that I'm not coming over—this agent is better than either me or, for that matter, Faisal. It took a bit of work at this end, had to rearrange a few cases, but you're not going after these perps without the best at your side."

"I appreciate it," Emir said, and the call ended seconds later. There was nothing more to say.

For now, all he could do was wait. He began to pace.

Somewhere over the Atlantic
Monday, September 14, 9:00 a.m. GMT

K. J. GELINSKY'S LONG legs were stretched in front of her and a cup of coffee sat at her elbow. Jackson, Wyoming, was a long way away and yet only days ago she'd been admiring the view from her apartment window, still in awe of the mountain peaks that cradled the city. Now the only view was the blind that covered the jet's window and hid the endless expanse of the Atlantic. At another time she would have soaked up the luxury of flying on such a plane, the decadence of being the only passenger with a flight attendant just a call-bell away. She'd been with Nassar Security for a little over a month and their use of private jets was still a novelty.

No expense had been spared to get her on a jet and flown over the Atlantic at a moment's notice. Briefly, she considered the resources of the men who owned both the agency in Wyoming and in Marrakech.

She'd met only Faisal and then only briefly. But she'd liked him immediately. His youth had surprised her. But, at twenty-five, only the snowboard he'd carried under his arm when she'd met him unexpectedly in the parking lot had indicated anything other than what he was: a serious business owner. He'd welcomed her to the team and put the snowboard down to shake her hand with the cordiality she'd later heard he offered to all his employees.

Faisal was approachable, friendly—the opposite of what she'd heard of his oldest brother who was rarely seen, at least by the Wyoming branch of the agency.

With only hours before wheels to the ground in Marrakech, she was anxious to get started, intrigued by the assignment and more than curious to meet Emir Al-Nassar. The head of the Moroccan branch of the agency, Emir, and his twin, Zafir, were the reason the agency had expanded as rapidly as it had. Emir was a friend to the man she directly reported to, which was interesting in itself, as were Adam's words as she'd prepared to leave. "He is one of the few people on earth I would trust completely."

This assignment was a coup for any agent. She'd been lucky that both her skill set and the fact that she'd been in New York on the last day of a training session had placed her as not only the logical choice but four hours closer than she'd normally have been.

She pulled her thoughts back to the case. The fact that she would be working with Emir and what kind of man he might be was irrelevant. What recognition she might get from her employers, the potential boost to her career, also moot points that only clouded her thinking. And yet they were very valid moot points. This case would—could, she amended—be career-making. She emptied her mind, bringing herself into a state of meditation for a few minutes.

Fifteen minutes later she was centered and focused on one thing: finding Sheikka Tahriha Al-Nassar.

On the tray in front of her was everything she knew and everything she might need to know about the case. She'd been through much of it already. Now she scrolled through the pictures Adam had just sent her. She memorized the features of the kidnapped sister, but it was the picture of her oldest brother that wouldn't leave her mind. Despite the fact that he was the president of the company, she'd never before seen a picture of him. She'd known that he and his brother Zafir were twins, but she hadn't known they were identical. She'd never seen either of them in person. Adam had provided her with a picture of each of them, for although it was Emir she'd be working with, they were all in Marrakech awaiting her arrival.

She clicked on Emir's picture, noting the difference that ran deeper than the length of their hair—Emir's shorter than his brother's, clipped above his ears. The difference was in the depth of his piercing brown eyes. She kept going back to his picture and told herself it was part of this assignment to know who she was meeting at the other end. But that was only part of the truth. Emir had an aura about him, a powerful sense of confidence that seemed to emanate from the picture.

K.J. closed her eyes. Despite her mind-focusing meditation, a nap would help her hit the ground running. But that wasn't an option. There was more to be done. She needed to know everything they had on the Al-Nassar family.

Despite working in the office headed by Faisal, she'd had little contact with him or his family, and now it was critical to fill in those gaps, along with learning everything about today's Marrakech. The last time she'd been in Morocco had been five years ago. She needed to familiarize herself with not only present-day Marrakech but also with the surrounding area if she was to get Sheikka Tahriha safely home.

She remembered the conversation just before she had taken off.

"There's been a payment," Adam had said in his

usual, abbreviated, no-intro sort of way. "Hopefully that will hold them off."

"You've advised that no more payments are to be made."

"Emir is well aware of that." Adam paused, clearing his throat. "One other thing. Be careful. A woman in rural Morocco—" he shook his head "—I'm taking a chance on this."

"I know. Don't worry, Adam," K.J. had said with a confidence she hadn't felt. It might be the twenty-first century, but this was the land of sheiks where ancient traditions and strict religious laws governed much of day-to-day life, especially in the rural areas where it was highly possible the kidnappers had fled to. She'd considered that and brought tops with long sleeves, and long pants. She'd also be sure to secure her long hair before she landed so that it was away from her face. Still, she knew it wasn't enough. But it was the best she could do. Her knowledge of the area would be her best defense. And if they wanted the best, she thought with more self-awareness than conceit, they would have to take her as she was.

She scrolled through the additional information. Then, she set down the tablet and lifted the paper report and skimmed through the pages. The report didn't give her a lot of hope. The kidnappers weren't sophisticated, judging from the trail of evidence.

Thugs were more difficult to reason with. In some instances, thugs couldn't be reasoned with at all. She feared that, in this situation, that might be the case.

Chapter Two

Emir glanced at his watch. Adam's last text told him that the investigator was thirty minutes away from landing. It was 2:30 p.m. and, according to the evidence, Tara had been missing for over twelve hours. Time was slipping away and yet there was nothing he could do beyond what he already had. Now, he waited, and only his iron-clad will kept him from taking charge of this case alone. That, and the knowledge that emotion had already colored his judgment.

The airport was crowded with people and luggage as commercial airline queues filled up and passengers waited for their flights, oblivious to his inner turmoil or to the fact that his family was in dire straits.

Emir strode through the crush of incoming passengers emerging from one flight and into a back room where few were admitted, to the security area where the pulse of the airport was monitored on a second-by-second basis.

"How much longer, Sihr?" he asked the man who

had first become familiar to him in the aftermath of the horror of the car crash that had killed both his parents six years ago. It had been here where an emergency crew had taken off in the hope of airlifting survivors from the isolated mountain road, and this man who had facilitated the quick takeoff. Emir ran a hand over his chin as if that would dispel the memory of a tragedy that had changed everything. Instead, all he felt was stubble and a reminder that time was slipping away.

He went over the expected time of arrival in his mind juxtaposed against weather conditions. As an amateur pilot he knew that, despite Adam's report fifteen minutes ago, flight conditions could easily have changed the plane's arrival time. "Early?"

Sihr gave him a brief nod. "It's landing now." The lean, middle-aged man swept his arm toward the back of the small office. "We can go out this way and meet them at the gate."

Emir was three steps ahead of the smaller man as he strode down a narrow corridor that turned into a common area used only by security. They were in an area that was off-limits to the average passenger, but not to Emir. Despite the fact that he had come to know Sihr during one tragedy where rules had been bent, despite the fact that his family employed Sihr's brother, being allowed into the security area wasn't a favor, at least not one in the traditional sense. It was how things were done for him, his family and those around him. It was how it had always been.

As they made their way through the bustling security area and Sihr opened a door that led directly to the runway, a small breeze hit him. That was immediately overlaid by the smell of jet fuel and the roar of a commercial airliner taking off that erased the chance of any conversation even if Emir had felt like starting one. He did not. He had nothing to say and nothing that Sihr needed to know.

To the left, a Gulfstream jet had just landed and was taxiing toward them.

"Security will clear them on the tarmac. Barring anything unexpected, you should be able to go straight through," Sihr said in his brisk, business-first manner.

Emir nodded. That bit of information was unprecedented for a foreign-origin aircraft and he knew it was Adam's doing. Their investigators traveled the world, sometimes disguised as normal tourists, and each time clearance was negotiated before the jet took off.

One passenger got off the jet. He waited. No one else appeared. He frowned, unsure of what was going on and yet sensing something wasn't right. His gaze traveled back to the passenger. She was a good-looking woman. He could tell that even from this distance. She was blond, her hair short or pulled up and away from her face, it was hard to determine which and none of it mattered. Still, he continued to watch as a security agent ran a wand down one side of her, skimming shoulder to ankle. Emir's gaze shifted away, uninterested—waiting for the investigator K. J. Gelinsky.

Minutes passed and then she was in front of him. She only had to tip her head slightly to catch his eye; a tall woman with a forward attitude. He took a step back, taking her out of his personal space.

"Mr. Al-Nassar," she said, holding out a slim hand. "I'm K. J. Gelinsky."

"Emir," he said almost by rote for "mister" had been his father and that era had ended in tragedy over half a decade ago. But even as he responded, the thoughts were shoved to the background as the reality of what she had said hit him.

"K.J.," he repeated as if he needed the repetition to commit the initials to memory. Something inside froze as he realized what Adam had done—what he would have said if Adam had told him the sex of the investigator beforehand. Adam would have known how he would have reacted. He would have known that this meeting would never have happened. He didn't offer her his hand. He couldn't.

"You're the new agent?" he asked, the words heavy with disbelief. "You're the one Adam recommended?"

"Yes," she said brightly. "I'm K.J.—"

"This won't work," he said. His thoughts were

clouded with anger at the thought of what Adam had done, of how much time might be wasted, and of Tara whose life would be further endangered now that there was no help forthcoming.

Her wide, smoky-blue eyes narrowed. "By 'this,'" she said slowly, "you mean me?" She took a step forward. Now she was in his face.

He frowned. If she were a man that would have been a mistake. But she was no man.

"That's what you were meaning, wasn't it? I'm not a man so…" She let the remainder of the sentence hang.

He paused long enough to take a breath to control the anger that made him want to lash out at someone, anyone. "You need to get on the first flight home," he said through clenched teeth.

"Give me a chance." There was no hesitation in her voice or in her stance as she faced off with him, her head up, her eyes sparking as if enjoying the challenge.

"It's not me that's the problem or needs to give you a chance," he said. All he could feel was the pressure of an invisible clock ticking and the betrayal of a friend thousands of miles away. Adam knew the customs, the inherent sexism that still wove through the ancient traditions of the desert tribes. He knew it all and, still, he had sent her.

"I know," she interjected. "It's the customs, the tribes outside the city, the—"

"It won't work," he interrupted, thinking of the desert and where he suspected Tara's kidnappers were hiding. He'd always been an equal opportunity employer and supported his sister, Tara, in her fight for change. It was a man's world. It didn't matter how much he disliked the fact, it was a truth that, for now, wouldn't change.

"Look, I know what I'm getting into. I'm qualified," she said, her bag swinging from her shoulder, her eyes bright with passion. "I specialized in Middle Eastern studies—an exchange student." She waved one delicate, well-manicured hand at him.

Just looking at that hand confirmed every doubt he had. It wasn't just about customs, she was female and because of that and so many other things, she was the wrong person for the job.

"I'll help you find your sister. You just need to trust me."

"No!" The word came out with all the pent-up fury that had built since the fateful call from Tara's kidnappers and now the full impact of it sparked in his eyes as his temple pounded and his fists clenched.

"No," he said with less edge but with no room for negotiation. He was wasting time, had wasted time, first waiting and now in a senseless airport run. "I don't care what you specialized in. You're a woman and because of that you're going home," he said bluntly. "I've wasted enough time. I'll speak to the pilot and we'll get you out of here."

"You're not being fair."

"I'm not being fair," he repeated, emphasizing each word. If she'd been a man he would have had her by the collar up against the wall, his face in hers. But she wasn't and that was the problem. "You're useless to me. I'd have to watch out for both you and me. That's a distraction. Look at you—you couldn't swing a punch or..."

One minute he was seething, glaring at her, and the next he was flat on his back.

"You bloody flipped me," he snarled, leaping to his feet.

"As you can see, I know martial arts as well as being an excellent marksman."

"Do that again," he said in a slow, measured tone, "and you'll wish you hadn't."

"That's it?" she asked, one eyebrow quirked. "That's all you've got?"

"This isn't going to work. None of it matters. Whatever your skill set, it comes down to you're a woman. Useless to me in this environment."

"You don't have a choice. It's me or no one," she said and glared at him.

His jaw clenched.

"Oh, and by the way, your attitude about women sucks. I feel for your sister."

"Keep Tara out of this," he snapped, realizing it was a ridiculous thing to say when it was all about Tara.

"This might not just be about money. I think you already suspect that."

He held his surprise back. He hadn't expected that; it was an idea he and Adam had only briefly touched on.

"Adam told you."

She shook her head. "Tara is the heart of your family. Without her, it's broken."

She was bang on and he wished she wasn't for it changed everything, including his decision to send her home.

"These could be men with a grudge against the House of Al-Nassar. After all, your family has a long and deep history in Morocco. Someone has more than likely been hurt along the way. What better opportunity than a chance to bring you down by taking the sister you and your brothers adore and bleeding you for some cash." She shrugged. "Simplistic, I know, but not improbable."

"Don't make me sorry," he said, hoping that by not escorting her back to the plane he wasn't making the biggest mistake of his life.

"There's no time to waste," K.J. said, swinging around and striding ahead of him. She didn't stop talking and her comments trailed behind her.

With no choice but to follow, he did, even as his eyes drifted downward and he found, in spite of the situation, that he couldn't take his eyes off the endless length of her legs, which were enticing despite the fact they were covered by faded, beige-cotton pants. That and the generous curve of a hip only confirmed that in no way could she be mistaken for the man he had only minutes ago hoped she was. He pulled his gaze away. He was engaging in exactly the kind of behavior he abhorred and the behavior his sister, Tara, would have berated him for. No playful calls of "it's a guy thing" would ever quiet her criticisms and attempts to get him and his brothers to toe the line. But all of those looks and comments in regard to the opposite sex, at least in Tara's presence, had only been made in jest, brotherly teasing of a sister they all adored.

"The first twenty-four hours are critical," K.J. said over her shoulder, as if telling him something he didn't know. She stopped, pivoted on one heel and faced him with more determination on her face than he'd seen on anyone in a long time. "You know that time is a luxury you don't have and I'm a problem you didn't factor. That's why you're angry, and I don't blame you."

The admission and her logical, calm attitude in the face of what he knew had been insulting, even contentious words, surprised him.

"Whether you want me or not, I'm here. There's no time to get a replacement and I have knowledge you don't have and objectivity that you desperately need. I believe that's why you made the call to bring me here. Am I right?"

"What do you know about the Middle East other than your studies?" The words revealed all the disdain and upset he was feeling. "What experience do you have?" Her education meant nothing. It wasn't experience and therefore, to him, not real. "You grew up—" He was going to say in Midwestern America; the truth was in the way she said certain words.

"Morocco." She cut him off and he guessed she was being deliberately vague. He could hear the edge in her voice.

"Really?" he said and didn't soften the sarcasm that laced the word.

"Really," she repeated and turned to face him. "At least, a few years anyway. Six years total—as a child and then a number of years in my last years of high school." She seemed to draw herself taller. "My father was an economic counselor in the American Embassy in Rabat. A few years later he returned, accepting another position in the Moroccan Embassy." She eyed him with a challenge in her eyes. "Are you done?"

His jaw tightened. She was right, there was nothing more to say.

"Good," she said and began to walk away then stopped. "By the way. Call me Kate." She threw that over her shoulder as if it were an afterthought. "One phone call?"

"So far."

She stopped.

"So the call came in shortly before 4:00 a.m.?"

"Correct. I alerted Adam immediately and got a plan in place. Apparently that was a mistake."

His phone beeped. He pulled it from his pocket and looked at it for just a split second as dread roiled through him.

"Yeah?" he snapped and then his hand stilled as his pulse seemed to speed up. He couldn't believe their audacity and knew it didn't bode well for them to have contacted him twice in such a short period. They weren't following a normal pattern. "You've been paid, release..."

Kate shook her head, mouthing something at him. He didn't know what it was, didn't care. He needed to focus on this, on what the kidnappers wanted and on how to get his sister out of their clutches.

"Put him off," she mouthed.

He gave her a brief nod. It wasn't anything he didn't know but at least it was confirmation they were on the same page. "I can't get it together right away."

The call ended shortly after and somehow during that brief time he and K.J. had formed a shaky alliance. "This time they want a quarter million," he said to her. It was double what they had first asked for and it was nothing in the scope of what his family was worth.

"By when?"

"Forty-eight hours or they'll kill her. There was no drop information."

"This is their second request and you paid them once."

He stopped, surprised, and then realized that Adam would have told her.

"You negotiated with them successfully." She nodded approval. "That's promising. I suspect they're a fragmented group but, even so, they're testing your limits, prodding you, making you more vulnerable by not giving you the drop site, making you worry."

"Making me react emotionally."

She nodded, as if his response were normal. "The next contact should give us a drop. They have their initial demand, still I doubt if they'll chance playing it out any longer. And that call? They were tormenting you—nothing more."

He thought of what he had done in those first desperate hours when he'd heard his sister was missing and what his first thought had been to do now, but there'd been no drop site and Kate was right. She knew her stuff. It was clear in her perception and instant analysis of what had transpired in the short time in which they had been together.

"Surprised?" she asked with a smile that was more a lifting of her lips as no emotion showed in her beautiful yet deadly, intelligent eyes. "Small. Unorganized." She wiped a strand of hair that had escaped her ponytail from her face. "Not so much unorganized as brought together temporarily for a common goal. What I mean is…"

"This isn't what they do regularly. They have no cause."

"Exactly. I would say that they're rough men needing money. Colleagues of some sort…"

"And none of that matters."

"All of it matters. We need their profile to get in their heads, find out who they are, to ultimately find Tara and get her out safely."

She was right and he didn't want to admit it. Yet he was beginning to believe that, despite his doubts, what she had in her head, the profiling ability she spoke of, would be invaluable in finding Tara.

"Satisfied?"

He nodded, his mouth set. "But you do what I say, especially if this takes us, like I suspect, into the desert."

"Thanks," she said pertly, an edge to her voice.

He had no idea if that was a yes or a no. The only thing he was certain of was that she was staying.

"Let's get going," she said briskly. "I need to be briefed on everything that's happened since you last spoke to Adam and anything you might not have told him." She looked at him with eyes that seemed to rip through the protective layers that shielded his emotion from the world. "I need everything."

But as she said those words they emerged into the crowded main area of the airport and nothing was said as they made their way past a queue of passengers dressed in everything from blue jeans to sundresses and burkas. The crowd thinned near the doors leading to the outside, where the air was thick with the scent of the heated rubber of airplane tires and exhaust fumes.

The driver had them loaded and they were leaving the airport within minutes, but it was as they exited the airport and a few miles away that chaos erupted.

Chapter Three

"Dell," Emir said to the driver of his Hummer. He put his hand on his shoulder. "This is K. J. Gelinsky, she's here to help us get Tara back." He turned to Kate. "Dell's a good friend. He's had my back more times than I can count." He knew that didn't explain everything to Kate but it gave her a reason to trust this newcomer.

The big, blond, broad-shouldered man had a grim look that, combined with his size, made most people back away. But despite that, his unsmiling face and rather utilitarian brush cut, there was a warmth about him few people except his close friends ever saw. His distinctive look with his bleached-blond hair was a striking contrast to his swarthy complexion, but no one would dare comment on the look, for Dell's size intimidated most people. Emir knew Dell could be deadly but he also had a soft spot for women, children and cats. In fact, he'd seen the big man stroke a tabby, murmuring to it like it was a baby.

"K.J.?" Dell asked her as if hinting there should be more to her name than just initials.

"K.J.," she agreed with an easy smile and a "don't mess with me" look in her eye.

Emir bet there were few people who called her Kate. It wasn't anything she had said but rather the way she owned the initials and the odd way she had looked when he'd called her Kate despite her having given him permission. He wondered why she'd allowed him the privilege. Was it merely because he was her boss or…? Whatever the reason, it was irrelevant under the circumstances.

He still had reservations about her. There was no proof of her abilities other than an expertise in martial arts and what Adam had said. Despite that, he had to admit there was something in her demeanor, a confident air, that took the edge off his doubts. She acted like someone who knew the Moroccan culture, exactly as she had claimed, and she moved with the fluid ease of a local, regardless of her foreign look. None of it mattered. The only thing that did was that she could do the job and that, with her, they could bring Tara home.

But something was off. Oddly, it wasn't doubts about Kate that had him on edge. It was something else and he knew she felt it, too. The ease he had felt radiate from her in the airport and even just now, when she'd met Dell, was gone. Now she was tense, her attention taking in her surroundings.

As he looked at her, a silent communication leaped between them. Yet there was nothing tangible, no action to take, and he didn't feel comfortable with that. He could see that she was equally as disconcerted. Her brow was furrowed and her hand was on the seat in front of her, the other on the holster of her gun. He suspected that she, too, was considering the possibilities of a threat that might not yet be visible.

He leaned forward.

"What's going on?"

Dell shook his head. His attention was focused on the road but a tendon in his neck stood out and his grip on the wheel was tighter than required for the driving conditions of a low-traffic road bordering the outskirts of the city. Tension seemed to run through the vehicle. "I don't like that Rover," he grumbled. "Don't ask me why."

The Land Rover was the only vehicle besides theirs on the road. It was ahead of them, having turned in from a side road only minutes ago. From the moment it had moved in front of them there seemed to be an instinctive reaction by everyone in the Hummer. It was a feeling that was common in the field, one he'd discussed with his brothers and one they had all agreed had validity. Instinct was what many modern men ignored and one in which the Al-Nassar brothers and their associates had committed to never sweeping aside. In fact, it was what

had been the difference between success and tragedy on a number of occasions.

Other than the fact that it was moving slowly
along the road, there was nothing overtly threatening about the Rover. The back window was tinted
and they couldn't see inside. That fact alone had
Emir moving his hand to the shoulder strap beneath
his jacket and the reassuring feel of gunmetal.

He looked at Kate. She didn't look at him, but
instead her attention was riveted on the steel-gray
Land Rover. Something was off and he didn't like it.

"Why in Allah's name are they moving so slow?"
Dell asked, his voice troubled.

"Something's not right." Kate pulled her Colt from
its holster.

"I'm going to pull back," Dell said as the Land
Rover maintained its rather slow speed, as if taunt-
ing them to pass.

In the Hummer the tension had just moved into
overdrive, everyone poised for a threat that had yet
to be determined.

The silence in the Hummer was thick. Emir
glanced at Kate. There was no give in her posture
and her jawline and lips were tight, her eyes focused
ahead, her gun in her hand. Tension seemed to tick
between them like a bomb about to explode. His finger twitched. Behind them was a stretch of empty
road, but that could change at any moment.

Without warning the Rover stopped and Dell had

no choice but to hit the brakes or go around. Without a backward glance to see if they were on board with the decision, Dell put the Hummer in reverse, taking them away from the Land Rover.

Emir's instinct sent prickles down his spine. None of this made sense. His eyes were fixed on the vehicle ahead of them that was now flipped around so that it blocked the road.

"What the...?" Dell reached for his gun and the driver's door almost at the same time as their vehicle stopped. "They're blocking us."

He had no worries about Dell, who, as a former soldier in the Moroccan military, knew how to not only take care of others but how to take care of himself. It was the guidelines Emir had used to hire many of his security and why it had been such a shock to hear of Tara's kidnapping. He'd surrounded her with the best.

His hand was on the door handle and his other pulling his gun from its holster when a shot was fired from someone in the Rover. It narrowly missed Dell. They'd been right to suspect trouble, but they hadn't been quick enough to avoid ambush.

Kate flung her door open almost simultaneously with Emir as he leaped to the ground on the other side, using the door for cover.

Out of the corner of his eye he saw her crouch before she jumped to the pavement and fired, taking out the Land Rover's left rear tire, crippling it.

Emir moved forward, keeping his head down as he used their vehicle for cover. Ahead of them, the passenger door of the Land Rover hung open. He peered over the edge of the hood of the Hummer and saw what looked like a hand, the black metal of a gun gleaming over the door. He fired, one shot and then two, and ducked down.

Silence.

He glanced behind him, mindful of their proximity to the airport. There was the possibility that at any moment innocent travelers could be heading out of the airport and directly into the line of fire. And almost as bad, possibly worse, there could be police. They didn't need the confusion or the procedures of police involvement complicating the situation and taking valuable time away from the search for Tara. This was their business and no one else's. He gripped his gun grimly, determined to end this and end it soon. Whoever these renegades were, they were obviously out of sync with what was going on and, more obviously, by the law of coincidence, somehow involved with Tara's kidnappers.

He took in the scene in front of him, the threat and the results of the threat that still remained. Twenty-five feet ahead and to the left was a body. He dove, taking cover as gunshot sprayed over the pavement. A glare from the passenger side momentarily blinded him as sunlight sparked off the metal of the opposing weapon and confirmed that someone was still alive.

"We want at least one of them alive," Kate said. She had moved around to his side and behind him. "I've counted two. Not giving us good odds," she muttered, "that we don't easily kill them both."

It was the ideal situation but it was also hard to control. The most they could ask for was that he, Kate and Dell came out alive. That was mandatory. Emir refused to accept anything else. He set the bar high when it came to keeping his employees safe.

Another shot was fired. This time it was clear that the weapon was different. It was a handgun. He'd seen the glint of the short barrel and then nothing—a single shot and silence. It was hard to tell how many there were. He wasn't as sure as Kate that there were only two. No more than three, he suspected, but they were keeping down, out of sight. So far there was no visual, so he couldn't pinpoint it.

A shot from the passenger side and then another and as he raised his gun. It was obvious that the choice to keep one of their attackers alive might not be theirs to make.

Emir fired and the man's gun clattered to the pavement, but no body followed. Instead the passenger managed to fling himself into the driver's seat even as Kate fired again and again. The Land Rover peeled away, veering right then left as the smell of burned rubber and gunpowder knifed through the air before the Rover careened to a stop about four hundred feet away from them. The vehicle listed slightly to the left with one tire flat and its right side jammed against an embankment of dirt and discarded cement.

"Stay here," Emir said to Kate.

He nodded to Dell. "Cover me."

But as he came up to the vehicle, there was no movement. The Rover had pitched on its side. The smell of gas permeated the air. Emir moved to the right, away from the driver. Everything was still. He inched along the driver's side where the man was slumped. Dead, unconscious or feigning—it wasn't clear. The only thing that was clear was that he wasn't moving and that, for now, he didn't pose a threat. Still, one couldn't be sure. Emir held his gun in one hand and pulled the driver's door open as he jumped back, both hands on his gun.

Nothing.

He moved forward, jammed the gun in the man's ribs and took a closer look.

"Dead," he muttered.

"Bad luck," Kate said as she came up behind him. "Or not." She held her handgun in one hand, her other free. "He probably wouldn't have given you anything, anyway, whether he knew where she was or not. You know that. It was all a long shot," she said matter-of-factly.

Emir looked at her. He wasn't surprised that she was there. Somehow, despite his command to stay, he had known she would back him up. In an odd way, it both infuriated and pleased him. The thought ran through his head even as he assessed the truth of what she'd said. It was clear that, somehow, in some way, these men were connected with his sister's disappearance. Otherwise, none of it made sense. Now it was possible they might never know how they were involved or, more importantly, what they might know.

She moved past him, poking her head into the vehicle, looking at the corpse, her movements quick and decisive as she went through his pockets.

He went up beside her. "Any ID?"

She shook her head.

"We don't have a lot of time and we don't want to get caught up in the bureaucracy of airport security." He looked back to where their vehicle sat and then above, where the roar of an approaching plane reminded them of the nearness of the airport.

Over two hundred feet away the man who had been on the passenger side lay sprawled on the pavement. With no thought to Kate, assuming only that she'd follow, he sprinted back the way they had come, his long legs easily covering the distance between the two vehicles. He heard Kate behind him, her breath coming in short puffs, and whether she could keep up or not—for now, it was not a consideration.

He stopped by the body, bending to get a closer look, but it lay facedown. He turned it over—male, he already knew that, and there was nothing unique about his clothing. The passenger had been thirty or so, and was dressed to blend in, in brown cotton trousers and boots. Like the man they had just killed, his T-shirt was brown, as well, and it, too, had no identifying markings. There was nothing but a slim gold ring on his right hand that might be used to identify him.

Emir eased the corpse down after a quick check of his pockets and gave him a final once-over, this time only with his eyes, looking for clues they might have missed. He stood. He hadn't expected answers but he had hoped that there would have been something—one clue that might bring him closer to finding Tara.

"Who are they? It makes no sense that they would attack us."

"You're assuming this is connected?"

"Aren't you?" She looked at him as he grimly nodded agreement.

Kate bent and pulled something from the man's shirt. She held it up. "Camel hair. This guy's been outside the city, and recently."

He took the small wad of coarse hair from her. It was more than likely camel—the texture, length and color was right—but what did that mean in a country where camels were common? "There are camels in Marrakech. Camels everywhere—this is Morocco," he said as if it was a fact that needed pointing out.

He wasn't making fun of her or, for that matter, even contradicting her. The blood seemed to roar in his ears. He wasn't thinking straight, hadn't been since Tara disappeared. He had to get it together and, in an odd way, despite their initial meeting, he was counting on Kate. His eyes met hers and he could see something troubling in their depths. He knew she was considering what he had said and more.

"True," Kate said. "But he's not the type to own one." She lifted a hand and turned it palm-up. She ran a thumb along the tips of his fingers. "Too soft. There's no evidence he worked with his hands, other than with firearms." She laid the arm across the decedent's chest and straightened as she pointed to his boots. "Knock-off Ralph Lauren boots." She grimaced. "Not something a camel owner would have, but maybe someone who had been near one recently. Sand on his boots." She turned the sole of the boot sideways. "Not much, but I think he came from somewhere out there. Look, the leather is scraped, like he was walking on rough terrain, not city sidewalks." Her arm swept in the direction of the mighty Sahara Desert. "What brought him here?"

She glanced in the direction of the airport. "We need to get out of here before the police show up."

"You're right." He gave the scene a final once-over. These men weren't professionals and he'd bet neither were those who held Tara. The burning question was whether the two of them were connected and, if so, why had they targeted him? It seemed improbable. Why kill him and jeopardize a ransom? He glanced at Dell, who had been quietly listening to what they had to say.

In the distance the sirens from approaching emergency vehicles began to wail. They all headed back to the Hummer.

"Trouble. Let's get moving," Dell said as he motioned for them to get in.

Emir opened the rear passenger door and Kate slipped inside.

"None of this makes sense," Emir said as he sat beside Kate.

"Or it makes complete sense," she said softly.

They were silent for the next few minutes as the Hummer sped away, leaving the mayhem behind for the authorities.

Emir's attention was now on Marrakech's sprawling yet oddly elegant skyline as the vehicle turned from the rural landscape and headed back to the heart of the city.

THE SILENCE WAS thick over the next few minutes as the miles dropped behind them and distance separated them from the recent mayhem. While Kate appreciated the opportunity to mull over her theory without questions, she suspected that Emir, too, had theories with no solid answers and, like her, was mulling them over, trying to piece it all together, to make sense of it.

She looked at him, at the seemingly unfeeling line

of his lips and yet she knew, from the little he'd said, that he had to be worried sick. He cared for his sister, and he'd do anything to get her back. That he'd give his life—that he'd said and she was here to make sure that didn't happen.

Everything was still, quiet between them.

She noticed little things. His hands were thick, sun-bronzed, yet he had long fingers. His hands were like those of an artist mixed with those of a laborer. But none of what was in his hands matched the aristocratic planes of his face or… Her heart pounded just a beat faster—and her mind wrestled with distance, with control. This was not about lust or even like but about life and death. She was here to do a job.

"We need to do this silently and quietly. That means as few people involved or in the know as possible." She glanced at Dell. In the heat of battle Dell been a good addition. But finding Tara was a different matter. They had to be subtle and more people created noise, figuratively speaking, and could alert the kidnappers. Besides, she knew nothing of Dell. She didn't know if she could trust him, even though Emir did, or if she wanted to.

"Dell's ex-military," Emir said as he watched her attention turn to Dell. "We served together. He's going to help while he can. Don't question that or anything else I decide," he said, practically ordering her not to question him.

She didn't say anything. She didn't like it, but she'd see how it played out for now.

"I'll show you what we think is ground zero," he said as if that were the reward not for her success in the field but for her silence.

She looked at the tense way Emir gripped his handgun and the tight line of his jaw and saw pain, a strong man who was fighting not to break. He needed help and not just someone who wielded a gun, not just muscle—he needed someone who could think clearly, unaffected by the emotion he refused to admit. Emir, whether he knew it or not, needed her.

"Where they took Tara," he said.

And it was with those words that she found herself locked into the reality of going back in time with the dark and silently brooding Sheik Emir Al-Nassar.

Emir, she corrected, for she couldn't think of him as "Sheik." Sheik didn't fit the persona of the young and brash man beside her. He was a man she imagined could easily steal a woman's heart even after annoying her as deeply and maddeningly as he had her. He was also a man in the midst of a tragedy that, she'd instinctively thought from the moment she'd seen his name, would eventually lead her to the hinterlands of the Sahara Desert.

But it was the man, not the desert, that caused her to pause. There was something about Emir, a passion and an intensity that was different from any man she had ever known. And that scared her more than anything else.

Chapter Four

"I need a vehicle registration search," Emir said as he spoke to his contact. It was standard procedure, a first link to who or what these men had been—dead bodies didn't talk.

"Stolen vehicle," he said to Kate after he ended the call.

"Not what either of us hoped for."

He shrugged. "Did you expect anything else?"

She paused as if pondering the information. "It fits. Definitely not best case, but not a surprise, either. The vehicle makes sense but the attack itself seems like a piece that just doesn't fit. If the men who attacked us at the airport were originally with the kidnappers, why would they leave the group, come back and try to kill us?" She rubbed her thumb along the inside of her wrist, as if doing so would somehow provide answers. "They won't get money from a body. It makes no sense."

Emir looked at her. "I have three brothers."

She frowned. "They can still negotiate with one of your brothers." Her eyes met his. "Were they trying to kill you to ensure the others paid?"

"Maybe. I don't know."

As the Hummer slowed, Emir pulled out his phone and punched a series of numbers. The massive bronze gates leading to his home slipped smoothly open and Dell maneuvered the vehicle inside.

Emir slid the passenger window down.

"Heard anything?" A middle-aged man with a Beretta strapped to his waist and an AK-47 over his shoulder asked as he stepped out of the one-room stucco cabin that functioned as a guardhouse. Lines of worry etched his forehead and his lips were compressed in an angry line.

"I'm sorry, no," Emir said, his eyes on the guard as if some silent communication were passing between the two.

He could feel Kate's eyes on him and knew that it might seem odd to apologize about his sister's disappearance to his staff. It certainly wasn't the norm, but then, nothing about this estate had been the norm since they'd lost both a matriarch and a patriarch on the same day. After that, the rules of running a large estate had changed.

Many of his employees were also friends, especially of Tara. Tara was a favorite among the estate's staff and he knew they were worried sick about her.

She had the ability to touch the heart of everyone she met. Little things mattered to her, like knowing the birthdays of each employee. She could ask each of them about their families, the smallest details of their lives and call their children by name. Considering the number of staff in their employ, Emir had never been sure how she did it.

The guard's hand moved to the Beretta at his side, touching it almost reverently in an unspoken acknowledgment of solidarity.

"Rashad, this is K. J. Gelinsky. She'll be working with me to get Tara back."

Rashad gave a solemn salute and a nod.

"Pleased to meet you," Kate said.

"Been with the family twenty years," Emir said as the vehicle moved on.

"He has an alibi?"

Emir tensed. "Rashad is devastated by what happened to Tara."

"But he was questioned?" she persisted.

"He was at home with his family when it happened. There're a half dozen men who work with him, all of them with airtight alibis. Zafir questioned everyone, not just security."

"I'd like to see where she was taken."

"Of course…" Emir said, and couldn't help but admire the way she remained focused and calm no matter what was thrown at her. "On the outside, away from the main gate."

"We need to go back," she said.

"You're surprised I didn't stop there right away?" he asked at the slightly puzzled look on her face.

"No." She shook her head. "You were testing me." She looked at him, her eyes sweeping his face. "And, yes, I need to see where Tara was taken."

Dell's phone buzzed. A minute later he turned around with a troubled expression. "My mother just texted me. My father doesn't have long."

"Dell, I'm sorry…" Emir began.

Dell had offered to drive him as a favor between friends. Even with his father in hospital and the family gathered for those last moments, Dell had insisted on at least taking him to the airport. He suspected that Dell had sensed something off—and, as usual, that instinct, which had saved them a number of times on previous assignments, had been right.

"Don't be," Dell said as he opened the door and got out.

Emir got out of the backseat. Dell was obviously anxious to go as he handed the vehicle's keys to him. He looked over to see Kate slip out the other side and grab the small canvas travel bag that Emir remembered tossing into the backset at the airport, which seemed like a million years ago. He turned his attention back to Dell. It was a difficult situation and he wished that he could change things for his old friend.

Instead, he could only take the keys Dell handed him.

"Dad's had seventy good years. Meantime, you need to find Tara. If you need me, you know…"

"I know, man. No worries," Emir replied. Dell had been there with him not only today but after his parents' deaths, and while he and his brothers raised a sister who at the time had been a young teen.

Emir watched as Dell turned with a nod and headed toward a battered-looking Jeep at the edge of the long drive that led to the entrance of the property. He could feel Kate's presence beside him but he didn't look at her. He needed a minute to let his emotions settle. There'd been too much tragedy in too short a period of time.

The sky was cloudy and the temperature was in the high sixties, much lower than average. Somehow the air seemed even cooler. He looked over as Kate shivered.

"You all right?" Emir asked as he looked at her with more concern for her comfort than he knew he'd shown since she arrived.

"It's been a long day," she admitted. "I'm tired and just a little chilled," she said as she pulled a lightweight jacket out of her bag, the soft smell of coconut wafting around her.

If she'd been a man he wouldn't have worried about her comfort. Another reason why she shouldn't be here.

The masonry wall that surrounded the compound stretched out in front of them. They'd retraced their way on foot to the entrance of the compound, stopping seventy-five feet outside of it to a spot where Emir had been told his sister had been taken. Behind them, it was dusty and flat, a field that stretched into nothingness. Behind that, a public road ran about three hundred feet perpendicular to where they were. It was close enough that, had there been any traffic, the noise would have been disturbing. Ahead of them, rows of palm trees announced the entrance to the Al-Nassar compound.

"They took her with little fight," Kate said minutes later.

"How do you know that?" he asked. It wasn't something anyone else had seen. In fact, with one man dead and another in the hospital, it seemed rather a ludicrous pronouncement. A movement behind him had him turning around. On the public road, a thin, sun-bronzed man in T-shirt and faded jeans peddled past on a bike that pulled a small cart. Around them Marrakech spread out on both sides, the city seeming to glow as a result of the rich red clay that defined many if its buildings, whether the towers of a mosque or the walls of the city.

"Do you have the kidnappers' original message?" she asked.

"I don't know where you're going with this."

"Trust me," she said, holding out her hand.

He pulled his phone from his pocket, punched in a code and handed it to her.

She took the phone, listened and then hit Replay immediately after it ended.

"What do you think?"

"The voice isn't distinctive. It's male, but beyond that there's nothing. Midrange. No accent of any sort. Odd."

"Exactly what I thought," he said.

"Too bad we couldn't listen to the second. Compare."

"They were different. I'm sure of it," he said. Unfortunately there'd been no time to record that message.

She handed the phone to him.

"They used a knife," she said. She didn't wait for him to answer for they both knew that had been in the report. "Interesting choice of weapon. Silent, but it also takes surprise or strength, ideally both, to be effective. At least to do it quietly with little struggle."

"It was dark, past midnight. She was almost home and her security was taken by surprise."

"Will he make it?" she asked, referring to the man who was now in the hospital.

"I went to see him. He's critical." His fist clenched. "Ahmed was a good man—is," he amended. "He tried to help, to stop them. That's what I assume from how it all ended. He wouldn't have done otherwise." The thought of one of his employees so close to death was gut-wrenching. There wasn't anything about this case that wasn't. He cleared his throat. "And then he tried to help me, give me information…but he's in such rough shape."

Emir's voice was tight even to his own ears and he could still feel the pain of seeing someone he'd known for years struggling to live and yet still wanting to help. "Ahmed would do anything for Tara." He took a breath as if controlled breathing would somehow change how he felt. "It will kill her to find out what has happened to him." He stopped for a moment, trying to regain control of his emotions.

"He said something?" She looked at him with eyes alight at this new piece of information. "That wasn't in the report. You spoke to him after," she said, confirming what was already clear. "What did he say?"

He knew that she was anxious for a clue that would get this investigation on the road. They both were.

"He said 'desert' and then, the irony of it all is that the next words weren't clear, but it sounded like a name—Davar. I don't know what Ahmed was trying to tell me. He coded almost immediately after." He clenched his fists, his gaze somewhere over her shoulder, his mind back to that hospital room. "They were working on him when I left."

If what he'd heard and what he now suspected was right, the desert was where they needed to go. But the Sahara was a big place—it was like saying they were going to Europe.

"Emir."

Her voice was like a caress and he took a step away. His jaw tightened and he fought not to send her home then and there.

"I've never heard of it as a place. I imagine you ran a check of local surnames?"

"Nothing," he said. "Maybe I heard wrong. He was half mouthing—could barely speak." He shook his head.

"It will be sunset soon. We can't be heading out, not in the dark and with no idea where we're going."

"Agreed." But she didn't move. Instead she stood there, considering. "Was it a name—place name, I mean? And if so could it have been something close—not exactly what you heard?"

"I don't know. There hasn't been much time to examine the possibilities."

"You had to pick me up and then there was the small shoot-out," she said.

"Exactly," he said with a slight smile. "Thanks."

"For what?" She frowned.

"For at least an attempt at humor. Oddly, it helps." There was more that helped, but he feared it also distracted—her lithe figure for one...and most of all her sharp intelligence and quick wit. He was still going to tear a strip off Adam, but he felt slightly more confident than he had an hour ago.

"Can I see her quarters?"

"There was nothing—"

She cut him off. "Trust me."

"THIS WAY," he said.

Kate noticed that he didn't temper his pace. At six-one, he was only three inches taller than her, yet his legs covered distances quickly.

She strode beside him, thankful for long legs that sometimes made finding jeans a challenge. This time, they were a gift that allowed her to keep up as they headed toward the sprawling mansion that was a mix of old and new. The size and opulence was like nothing she'd seen in the working-class neighborhood of Detroit where, except for the stint in the Middle East, she'd grown up, or like Jackson, Wyoming, where she now lived. Her gaze swept the area, focusing on security details, potential breaches, rather than the opulence of the building and the grounds.

"There are sensors on the wall that monitor activity inside and out."

His arm swept the five-acre square where as far as she could see, a cream-colored masonry fence surrounded the complex's grounds.

"The cameras are on twenty-four-seven."

If Kate hadn't spent years immersed in Moroccan culture and, as a result, been aware of what "rich" in Morocco meant, she would have been pie-eyed with disbelief. This wasn't the wealth of royalty, and by no means a palace, but it was more than 90 percent of the population of Morocco would ever see.

She could understand why the security was as intense as it was and why Tara had been taken. The estate's opulence combined with their business, Nassar Security, added to riches that could be hugely tempting to anyone with a criminal bent. She knew the history of the company, knew that the twins had begun it and then, with the inclusion of their brothers, built a business that had taken on more high-profile cases than any other security company of its kind in either the western United States or Northern Africa.

"Interesting—about the security I mean." Her gaze met his. "And yet they took her at a place near where the cameras didn't reach."

His jaw clenched. "I'd planned to add security cameras there, too. But somehow it felt like overkill. Now, it's a glaring error."

"Cameras wouldn't have stopped—"

"No," he interrupted. "But alarms and—"

"You couldn't have known," she interjected as she tried to reassure him.

But the anger that emanated from him made it clear he didn't want reassurance.

"One of Tara's security is dead and the other, the only witness, is fighting for his life," Emir said. "It was an unforgivable lack of judgment on my part. I should have…" His voice dropped off as if he couldn't, or didn't, want to finish.

"What? Known? Are you psychic?"

"No, I don't believe…" He stopped and turned to look at her, his brow furrowed. "You were being facetious."

"The man who lived. He was knifed in the chest. I'd guess that he was defending her."

Emir shook his head. "He shouldn't have been there. Ahmed was estate security. He volunteered to go with Tara that night. It wasn't his usual job but one of our regulars called in sick."

"That wasn't in the file," she said.

"Like I said, some of the details weren't available, at least not then. I wanted an agent on the first flight here. I couldn't wait to fill in the blanks."

Nor could he wait to ensure the sex of the agent, either, she thought dryly, admonishing herself.

To be fair, after the opposition at the airport, he now seemed to have accepted her for what she could do and had at least stopped talking about sending her back because of her sex. It appeared that she was the only one who had yet to get over that faux pas, but in her mind it had been a big error. Enough, she told herself. She needed to focus on the key elements of the case.

"The security seems airtight. Explains why they didn't take her here," Kate said as they walked through the massive entrance that led to the Al-Nassar family home.

She glanced at Emir as he ran a hand down the dark stubble that covered his chin and jaw. He was an extremely good-looking man, but then, she'd known that. Now he looked agonized, worry lines creasing his forehead. She wanted to say something to comfort him but there was nothing that would help until his sister was home—safe. No matter what he thought, it hadn't been his error. It had been Tara's. His sister had made an error by ditching her security and that could cost her her life.

Still over a quarter of a mile away, she took in the scope of the house, more aptly a mansion, and its surrounding grounds and thought there was some irony in its sweeping size when only half the family lived here at any given time. She knew the majority of the family spent a great deal of time overseas. On most days she imagined that Emir was vastly out-numbered, not by family, but by the staff necessary to maintain such an estate.

"Emir?"

He looked at her as if he had been somewhere else. And she imagined he was fighting his own fear—fear for his sister's well-being and for her very life. He was too close emotionally and that was why he needed her. Her ability to move ahead without emo-tional attachment to the victim, his sister, whom she'd never met, was critical.

"And yet none of this security kept Tara safe," Emir said and both of them could hear the irony in his voice.

"You couldn't protect her night and day." She touched the back of his arm, the heat of his skin seeming oddly intimate. He tensed and she dropped her hand. "She's a grown woman."

From the corner of her eye she saw Rashad approaching.

"I'll run you up to the main house," Rashad said as he walked with them the remaining few feet to the guardhouse. He opened the door to the Hummer that Dell had so recently left, for Kate. His dark eyes were full of questions and yet he asked nothing.

Within minutes they were driving around a circular drive that had been hidden behind massive palm trees. They skirted a white-marble fountain that was devoid of water.

"Maintenance issues?" she asked Emir. "Your estate is immaculate and yet the fountain isn't working?"

"The plumber was called but I put the repair on hold."

She turned. "Anyone else who's been here recently? Aside from staff, I mean."

"No one, except the plumber two days ago," he said.

"Was Tara around when the plumber was here?"

"Yes, I believe she was. I don't remember her coming out of her quarters, though," Emir said. "The plumber had done work for me on numerous occasions. We've contracted him for years—in fact, I believe he worked for my father, too. Anyway, he didn't stay long. I decided against the repair. I hadn't planned to be here for this long."

"By here, you mean Marrakech?"

"Morocco, actually," he said. "If all this hadn't happened, I might have met you in Wyoming. I'd planned to go there. A recent case involving the Wyoming secretary of state's brother piqued my interest."

"Faisal will have his hands full. It's high-profile," Kate said. "So, plumbing is minor considering everything that's come down in the last week."

"You could say that." He shrugged as if it were all of no consequence while the tension around his eyes and mouth made him look almost feral, like a man who would protect anyone or anything whose heart belonged to him. She had to force her thoughts back to what he was saying.

"I promised Tara that when she was home for summer vacation, I'd have the fountain up and working. She finds it soothing."

"Was anything else happening that day or any day after?"

"Nothing out of the ordinary."

The Hummer stopped in front of the mansion with its huge columns and sprawling white-tiled front entrance.

She glanced back at Emir as she stepped out. She wondered if he felt like he'd been interrogated, for, without meaning to, she knew that was what she had done.

He stepped ahead of her to open the massive wood-and-brass door. In the seconds that it took, her gaze ran the length of his muscular back and she had to pull her eyes away from the lush, seductive curl of his dark hair as it flirted with the edge of his collar.

Get a grip, she told herself as she walked past him and into a vast tile-and-marble area that stretched beyond the colossal entrance doors, eclipsing them in opulence. For a moment her reason for being here was clouded by her feeling of disbelief. Her life, her two-bedroom apartment, compared to this? The juxtaposition of the two realities wasn't even fathomable. This was a fantasyland, a different world that she'd known of but of which she couldn't have imagined until now. It was laughable, really, eight hundred square feet that she lived in compared to this. The comparison was as unstoppable as it was fleeting, rather like looking at a magazine rack and seeing one on budget travel lined up beside another that was geared to luxury resorts.

She pushed the thoughts out of her mind and instead considered everything this wealth brought—including the case she was now assigned to. She knew fortune such as this did not come without responsibilities. She also knew there were expectations here and duties Emir had inherited from his father, and even from his grandfather—a responsibility to the people, to give back. She knew Emir took his responsibilities seriously; she'd heard Adam speak of it. It explained why Emir seemed so contained, controlled—older than the thirty-one years she knew him to be.

She looked around, taking in the length and width of the area even from the entrance. The hallway seemed to stretch indefinitely and, rather than the chill one would expect from such a large space, the air was warm.

As they moved down the corridor she couldn't get over the size. The estate was massive, more imposing than she'd expected, both inside and out. There had been no available pictures, even of the grounds; nothing she could get from the internet. Oddly, even the area outside the gates hadn't been Google-mapped. She guessed that had been Emir's doing.

But it was the pictures some yards from the entrance that made her pause; they were the only decor in the hallway that stretched easily a half a city block. She stopped for a minute as she looked at a picture of a man and a woman, middle-aged— the woman looking younger and very much like the photos she'd seen of his sister, Tara.

It was odd that the pictures were here in this luxurious but barren corridor with the only other decor, the oval, brass entranceway doors facing them not ten feet away. "These are your parents?"

"Yes, taken only months before their accident. Of course," he added, "that was a long time ago."

Six years wasn't a long time ago. Was he distancing himself from the trauma of the loss? She supposed it didn't matter either way. What was important were the facts. She'd read about the traffic accident on a treacherous, isolated mountain road and the resulting fire that had tragically taken both Emir's parents.

"Tara looks very much like her mother." Kate stared at the picture as if the answer to saving Tara was somehow in the dark eyes of the beautiful woman who stared back at her.

For a moment she was caught by the woman's image. Her eyes reflected the same rich ebony as her eldest son. Her smile was the same as Tara's picture in the file she carried. But whatever answers or secrets those eyes might hold wouldn't be forthcoming from a picture.

"Kate."

Her name was a command as he waited for her to catch up. She was reminded of how few people called her that. Allowing Emir to call her by her given name had surprised even her. She'd gone by her initials since she was a child. She couldn't tell when or why it had begun, but the initials had served her well in the profession she'd chosen as an adult. Now, K.J. just was and it was odd that Emir had become one of the exceptions. At another time she'd have analyzed what that might mean.

She walked beside him, her pace matching his. White columns ran from the tiled floor to a ceiling that soared over twenty feet above them. Their footsteps echoed on the ceramic tile as they turned left and into another corridor as vast as the first. This one brought them to within fifty feet of another massive door not quite as large as the entrance and this time without the brass. Instead these doors were wooden with gold glittering in a heart design over both panels.

"Tara's apartment," Emir announced. "This was the women's area centuries ago," Emir said as if he'd seen the disbelief in her look and wanted to confirm what she already knew. "Tara thought it laughable to claim for herself this area that, a hundred or so years ago, was a harem." He shook his head. "She's always about being contrary."

"Contrary?" Kate frowned.

"I didn't mean that," Emir said. "We are all more Western in our thoughts—the family, I mean—but Tara wanted to change the thinking, the old ways, that exist elsewhere. Chauvinism that still hasn't disappeared. She wasn't content to let modern ideas remain within the walls of this compound or within the boundaries of Marrakech, for that matter."

The pain in his voice was palpable.

"We'll get her home." She met the troubled look in his eyes and hesitated, feeling the need to comfort. She dropped the thought when she saw the anger in his eyes. Anger was not something she could change with simple words or a touch and, at this stage, she suspected it would be unwelcome.

As they entered Tara's quarters, it was as if facts were his safety net as he commentated as they walked. "Built almost two hundred years ago, this area is pretty much impenetrable to outsiders. Always has been. We've upgraded, of course. This section was built in the mid-1800s. We've put in a computer-monitored surveillance system in the last few years, added motion detectors and thermal laser-heat detectors. It was all we needed without going overboard. At least, so we thought…" He shook his head, lines bracketing his mouth.

"You couldn't have known."

"Don't placate me," he growled. "I should have known. It was my job to know."

The security keypad was imbedded in a teak panel arched into a design that looked rather like a small pseudo door set alongside the door frame.

Emir punched in a code.

The doors in front of them opened with the whir of a hidden motor, leading to a smaller teak doorway and a wooden door that, while arched like the first set of doors, was smaller, singular and, as a result, much less imposing than the first set. Emir unlocked the door, flicked on the light and stood aside for Kate to enter first. Inside was the sleek metal lines and modernity of a penthouse apartment without the extravagantly opulent touches of the entranceway.

His hand was on the small of her back as she hesitated, taking it all in. Her heart beat just a little faster as his hand rested there for just a few seconds longer before the intimate touch was gone and it was as if it had never happened.

She was being ridiculous and, worse, unprofessional, she chastised herself, dragging her thoughts to what was important—learning about Tara and finding anything that might help to bring her home, safely, to her family.

"Tara detests the old look. It reminds her of the old ways and the customs that still impact women. She left some of the original touches, the original door and entranceway, because they amused or maybe, more aptly, intrigued her."

Kate walked the length of the cool, ivory tile that matched the rest of the mansion and straight through a kitchen and sitting area to a bank of windows that looked out to a gleaming infinity pool surrounded by palm trees. She turned back to Emir.

"If she wasn't so smart, this wouldn't have happened. She wouldn't have pushed the rules, tested her limits," Emir protested. "She'd have been inside and safe." His lips were taut, his eyes dark and troubled. Kate held back the urge to put a hand on his shoulder, to offer what little comfort she could.

"You can't turn back the clock," she said softly.

Her gaze went to the sofa as she walked over to the bookcase. "She's very serious," she said, her eyes skimming the titles. "And yet she has a lighter side, fun-loving." There were characteristics of Tara that were obvious in her choice of furnishings. The sleek, butter-yellow leather sofa hinted at a lighter side. The heavy, teak desk with generations of wear marring the surface and the three volumes of Wells's *The Outline of History* leaning against an economic text were testament to her seriousness.

Kate glanced at a collection of graphic novels but picked up an archeological magazine from a pile and thumbed through it. It was a unique collection for a young woman whose major was computer science with a minor in psychology. She put the magazine back on the stack that seemed to cover the prior year.

"Did she just read about archeology or had she gone on a dig?"

"What does it matter?" he asked.

"Anything you remember could help, you know that."

He nodded. "You're right. She wanted to go check out a new find. It was a day trip into the desert and another back."

"And you told her no?" Kate guessed and got her answer from his silence. "That must have been hard for her to take. Maybe impossible, considering she's legally an adult. Is it possible that she planned to go anyway, that maybe…?"

"No!" A minute of silence hung between them before he spoke again. "What are you implying?"

Tara picked up another magazine and thumbed through the pages, deliberately putting off her answer. It was best that he knew now, before this investigation went any further, that she wouldn't be intimidated. She also knew he was a hard man to convince, considering a gunfight hadn't done it.

She would have laughed if the situation hadn't been so serious. Instead she continued her perusal of Tara's living space, finding bits of information that would give her insight the file and Emir hadn't. Finally, after a minute had passed, and then two, she looked up, met his gaze and saw a hint of what might be admiration.

It was vital that she had his full attention. What she had to say could be very important to who, at least, some of the perpetrators might be. She didn't expect him to take what she was about to imply well, but it had to be said. "Is it possible that days or even weeks ago, she made first contact, made the culprits aware of her vulnerability?"

This time his look was thunderous as he turned away from her. The tension between them was thick and bleak before he turned back. Now his eyes glimmered with anger, agony—maybe a combination of the two, it was impossible to tell.

"Is that so unbelievable? I'm not saying it was her fault but only that…" She paused.

"Yes, it's possible. But I don't know anything more than I've already told you and what was in the report."

"What about that night? What wasn't in the report, Emir?"

"She was celebrating the beginning of the school year, getting together with some old school pals on a few days' jaunt home before going back to the States. And…" His full lips thinned and his jaw tensed, and she could see he was struggling with something.

"Sit," she offered with a wave of her hand to the chair opposite her.

He sat.

"I admit the report is missing some information. It wasn't all known. I learned it after your plane took off and—" he wasn't looking at her "—I've filled in all the blanks." He opened his mouth as if to say more.

She cut him off. "I need to know what Tara was doing last night—all of it."

"I…"

She met his rich, dark eyes, saw the trouble, the doubt, that lurked deep within them, and still she didn't back down.

"She left the restaurant alone with her security. She managed to ditch them shortly after—no one knows why." He blinked, as if that would change the words she knew, for whatever reason, he didn't want to admit.

"It won't help to hold anything back."

Silence ticked between them.

"The only thing that matters now is having all the

information so we can figure this thing out and find her. What aren't you telling me?"

"She'd been drinking," he admitted. "That's what her friends said."

"What else did her friends say?" she asked softly.

"I didn't want this in the report, it…"

"Could ruin her reputation." She paused. "Look, Emir, we've all gone there. A youthful mistake—a bit too much to drink. It happens. Usually it turns out well—we luck out. Let's make this turn out well. Tell me what happened. Everything you know, including what you screened from the report."

She looked at him as if he were no different from any other witness.

"You knew this before I left the States and you left the fact that she'd been drinking out of the report. You did that on purpose, thinking it didn't matter. It wouldn't change anything or help us find her."

She sank onto the luxurious softness of the leather couch and thought how she'd love such a piece for her small apartment. Then she turned her focus on Emir. "That's where you're wrong—and you know it. Everything matters, every piece of evidence."

He ran his hand along his brow and his gaze dodged hers. "I've never known her to overindulge. Her friends admitted it happened rarely." He looked at her as if daring her to say otherwise.

"A mistake that many of us have made at one time or another."

He shook his head.

"Where are they, her friends?"

"I've already spoken to them. They left her, from what I can determine, over an hour before she was taken. They didn't see her after that. That part is in the report."

"I read it," Kate admitted as she got up and went over to the window. She didn't remind him of what hadn't been in the report. Her fingers skimmed the window frame. "Bulletproof." She glanced at the door. She'd noted the hinges earlier; the door swung out rather than in, difficult for a man to break down. Not that it mattered. The crime had happened elsewhere.

"Let's go back to the airport and the attack," she said. "There's a connection, but what is it?"

He stood, pacing along the couch to the window and back, and then stopping a few feet from her.

"So we have two bodies and one gives us some clues," she said when she was met by silence. "Camel hair and his boots—the sand on them, it was caked, not something you get hanging around the city. I'd say he'd recently been in the desert. What better place to get lost in or to request a ransom and remain out of reach of detection? Even the best technology can fail against the might of the Sahara." She looked away as if regretting having to speak the words they both knew. Extracting Tara was not going to be easy.

"I can't argue with any of that," he said in his distinctly low voice. "It kills me to think of her frightened or in pain." He ran a hand through his dark hair that, despite the short cut, curled wildly and only succeeded in giving his sun-bronzed, chiseled good looks a rakish edge.

This was a difficult case, fraught with emotion and involving the man who was effectively her boss. And yet it was hard to think of him like that when, from the first moment she'd seen him, there had been a connection, an unseen emotion that seemed to pulse between them. She shoved the ridiculous thought from her mind. For now, he was her assigned partner and client rolled into one—nothing else.

Chapter Five

"So far the name Tara's injured guard gave you— Davar—doesn't exist. Not as a surname and a given name would be impossible to track. Even in the state he's in, Ahmed would have known that. No, he was giving us something we could find," Kate said. "I know we did an initial check, but I've gone beyond that search and been through everything. I've had the records of anyone who had a vaccination, a driver's license or even stepped foot in Morocco scoured. Nothing."

She ran one hand through her hair, bunching it in her hand and pulling the long, silken mass back and away from her face.

"Are you sure that was exactly right? He was mouthing the word, you said. Could you have misunderstood?"

"It's possible, but it's all I can get for now and, if it's not exact, it's close. He's in and out of consciousness," Emir said as a nerve caused his jaw to twitch.

Time was wasting and there was nothing they could do but wait and speculate.

"So we use what we have. Both time and evidence," Kate said as she perched on the edge of the massive rosewood desk that had been his father's. They'd left Tara's apartment and entered his office an hour ago.

He knew she was going over the possibilities of that one word, the name the injured guard had provided—Davar. Yet his attention went to her long legs that hung over his desk and the creamy satin of her neck as she leaned her head back against the filing cabinet that butted up to the desk. She had beautiful skin and, for a second, he imagined what it would be like to caress it.

And, as if she read his mind, Kate looked at him with determined eyes and lips that were soft, kissable. His thoughts were out of line, inappropriate and unproductive. But he couldn't seem to dodge them for, despite his outrage that Adam had sent a woman, he'd been drawn to her since the first moment he'd met her.

"We'll get her, Emir. We'll get Tara out and home safe. I promise." There was grit in her words. It was as though her saying them somehow made them true. He only wished it was going to be that easy.

He strode over to the window. The city sprawled out in front of him. It was the place where he'd been born and where he'd grown up—the city he'd thought to escape in his young adult years and the city that now seemed to promise the secret to saving his family.

The second call had been long enough to be tracked by their office team to within a twenty-five-mile radius of Marrakech. They'd received that information almost immediately after the call had ended. It wasn't enough. They were still looking for a needle in a haystack.

Kate was now pacing the room, a pensive look on her face. He knew they both felt the passage of time and the frustration of their current inertia, but there was no getting around it. Kidnap victims had died because of ill-prepared rescue attempts. He was determined that Tara would not be one of them. Behind them the office clock ticked, the dull beat of time a passing reminder of everything they could not do.

She looked at him, her eyes seeming to reach out to console, but he couldn't help noticing instead the long wisp of blond hair that had again escaped the elastic band and curled down her face, caressing her chin, bringing his attention to the soft, seductive rise of her breasts—

What was he doing? He needed to remain focused. His sister's life was at stake and he was letting a beautiful woman distract him. Again, he was reminded why a woman should not be there, why he should have held firm, why...

"No woman will voluntarily go with a man she doesn't know. Especially at night, in the dark," Kate said softly, interrupting his thoughts as he found she was apt to do. This time it had been a good thing.

Kate pressed her forefinger to her lips. "To take someone that quickly and easily, I believe there are only two scenarios that might work."

"She knew her captor," he said grimly.

"Exactly. Or she was tricked. A stray animal, a child needing help—another woman."

"I don't think anyone we knew would have done this," he said.

"You mean you don't want to believe that someone you know would do this."

She'd called him out again. He met her eyes, saw rock-solid determination, and knew she had his back.

"No matter, Emir. We have to consider all possibilities."

"You're right," he agreed. She was everything Adam had said she would be, except she wasn't a man. He was beginning to wonder if that mattered.

"I still think she knew them, was at least familiar with them," Kate persisted in a voice meant to get a man's attention and a mind that challenged him to keep up.

He pushed the distracting thoughts back and focused on what she had said. It was interesting she'd said "they" instead of "he." It was another possibility for which he had no answers. He turned to the window, squinting as the setting sun shone across the square, bounced off a distant, copper-topped bell tower and created a glare that was almost impossible to see against. Dusk was fast approaching and soon the call to prayer would taunt them, remind them of passing time. Normally patience was what he was good at, yet patience was what he found impossible to implement in the one case that mattered more than any other.

"Her guards were easily disposed of," Emir said.

"She might not have seen the violence. They might have been attacked without her even knowing. Then the perpetrator comes up to her, lures her, and she's not suspicious because she knows who it is."

The fact that Tara might have known the perpetrator, that someone he had given his trust to, could have betrayed him in the worst way possible almost took him out at the knees, even though the possibility was something Kate had alluded to earlier and one he'd considered himself. Now, for the first time, he was able to entertain an idea that had the potential to make this case, if that were possible, even more gut-wrenching.

"Emir?"

Kate's voice was calm yet husky in a completely feminine way. She'd taken him out, literally flipping him onto his back, but it was her voice he knew could be his undoing. Now it was all he needed to bring him from his thoughts and into her presence.

"When was the last time you spoke to Tara?"

"Yesterday afternoon. It was a quick call. She told

me that she planned to meet some friends—she mentioned the local nightclub. That was it." He shook his head, his eyes not meeting hers. He didn't need that distraction, that allure—he needed to focus and she was making it difficult. "All I told her to do was have fun. Instead, I should have…"

"Should have what, Emir?" Kate interrupted. "You're not psychic. You did what you could—better than most. She's a grown woman. She made her own decision and, unfortunately, the consequences were nothing anyone could anticipate. The only thing we can do now is get her home safe."

She was right. He needed to quit thinking in the past unless it was something that would help. Although Kate hadn't said any of that, he could read it in her tight stance, the accusing spark in her eye and the set of her chin. She wasn't putting up with any emotional swaying on his part. She was making him toe the line—and it was exactly what he needed. Ironically, he was the most unemotional of his brothers, the least likely to act on emotion despite the circumstances.

But the thoughts wouldn't be stilled as he contemplated the horrible thought that Tara knew her attacker. That the perpetrator who had planned this crime knew his sister. That he had her trust. It seemed more and more likely that that was the only thing that made sense.

Four questions—who, why, what and where—and no one had the answers.

He glanced at his watch. If his calculations were right, Tara had been gone for over fourteen hours.

They'd hypothesized enough. Time was running out.

AT THE SOUND of his voice, Tara cringed and pulled her knees up to her chest, as if making herself smaller would make her invisible. She pushed her back against the sand-crusted cliff.

"I should have never listened to him. Cousin or not, he's an idiot," the man said, continuing his one-person tirade.

She made herself look at him, at the horrid scar that brutalized one side of his face, at the dark hair slicked with gray—at the person who threatened her very life. She needed to find out everything she could to help her brothers get her out. She'd known since the beginning that this man was in charge. What was frightening was that he was no stranger to her. But he wasn't the man she remembered, either.

She watched as he wiped the back of his hand across his stubbled chin as another man, slimmer and taller, walked past. He muttered something and the man she had come to loathe, and who led them all, cuffed him across the back of the head.

"Stop that," he snarled. He spoke in his native Berber and it was unclear to Tara, and she suspected to the man he had just accosted, what it was he should stop.

Silence settled for a few seconds in the small oasis that had become her nightmare. She looked around, conscious that he was sensitive even to her silent scrutiny. She was doing as little as possible to draw attention to herself. The thought of her brothers is what kept her strong and would get her through this. But the leader's next words frightened her like no others could.

"I'll bring the bloody house of Al-Nassar to its knees." He chuckled, the sound as dry as the endless sand that swept around them, flirting with the boundaries of the only greenery for miles. "Soon I will be a rich man."

He turned so that he partially faced her as he coughed and scowled.

"What are you staring at?" he snarled.

"Nothing," she said with oomph in her voice. For the one thing she'd learned since her kidnapping was that the man she would now think of only as *he*, detested weakness.

She stared at him before he finally turned his back to her.

The word he snarled as he stormed away was as evil as all the others he'd cursed at her. She knew the anger wasn't directed at her but at the house of Al-Nassar and everything he thought it stood for. He'd made that clear in the first miserable hours when they'd taken her and all the hours since.

Tara breathed a sigh of relief and prayed, for she didn't know how much longer she could keep the evil at bay.

Chapter Six

Monday, September 14, 7:00 p.m.

They had agreed that there was nothing they could do until daylight. The Sahara wasn't welcoming during the day, never mind at night. There was no need to push the limits, especially as there had been no further communication from the kidnappers.

That worried Emir.

"The airport attack had to be tied to the kidnappers. But why?" Kate asked. "Something doesn't fit."

He paced and tried to ignore the pulsing headache. He'd already popped a couple of aspirin and an hour ago he'd admitted to himself that there was no hope for it, the headache was there until Tara was brought home unscathed.

"We should have gotten a final demand by now. None of this makes sense," he said, knowing it could make perfect sense. But maybe it all made sense and it was that last, unspoken option he didn't want to contemplate.

"Could their plans have gone somewhat awry?" Kate mused. "We were attacked at the airport by men who we believe were part of Tara's kidnappers, but why attack us?" She shoved her hands into her pockets as she paced the room. "They've got to be connected—the kidnappers and the airport attackers. And they had to have a motive for the attack. Is it possible they're working at odds with each other?"

Emir heard the reluctance to believe her own theory in her voice. Like him, she knew that if she was right, if there were problems among the kidnappers, that could only mean problems for Tara. It wasn't the usual kidnapping pattern, but for every norm there was the deviant. These kidnappers were obviously true deviants. And that only made him angry and fearful at the same time, fearful that they wouldn't find Tara alive.

"She'll be fine, Emir. We'll make sure of it."

He took a breath, focusing on what could be done now.

He had to think about practical things. Things that needed to be done by morning—gathering supplies that would see them through a journey into the desert. He'd already set staff to complete that task. But there were other things. They needed to eat, rest and prepare for what lay ahead.

Whether they heard from the kidnappers or not, whether her abductors returned Tara voluntarily or not, they would face justice and Emir would be the one leading that charge.

His stomach rumbled, reminding him of a more immediate problem. But already that problem was also on the edge of resolution. He'd sent word to the kitchen and ordered Moroccan omelets for both of them. It was a light meal enhanced with the subtle tastes of various herbs, tomato and onion, perfect for not making one so satiated that lethargy set in. They couldn't afford that.

There was movement in the doorway, followed by a hesitant knock.

He looked up and saw Baz, the son of one of his estate security. The teenager hesitated in the doorway as he held a tray of food Emir had ordered less than twenty minutes ago.

"On the desk would be fine, thanks." He eyed the boy. "You're off duty soon?"

The slight yet gangly, dark-haired youth nodded. "I'm sorry about Tara, I…" He dropped his head and backed up, his hands behind his back. "Can I help? Find her, I mean."

For the first time in hours, Emir had a faint urge to smile. It was a fairly public secret that the boy had a crush on Tara. But, at only seventeen, his youth combined with his current status in life—son of a guard—might mean that life wasn't going to throw him a chance at his sister's affections. Too bad. In a few years Emir thought it was a good guess that the boy would mature into a man who could make a woman proud. His jaw tightened. He wanted Tara to live to have the choice. He pushed the thoughts away and met the boy's concerned gaze.

"No. You don't want to intimidate them with too big a show of force," he said, flattering the boy. "We'll find her," he assured him as Baz nodded and left.

They ate their meal quickly and in silence. It was sustenance only and, oddly, a moment to collect their thoughts individually before they began brainstorming all over again.

"We've still got nothing but assumptions as to where they've taken her. For all we know, she could still be in the city, she might never have left," Emir said as he picked up their plates and utensils and set them on a tray Baz had left on a table by the entrance.

"I'm not so sure," Kate said.

She looked young and too fresh and pretty to have wielded a gun as efficiently as she did. He'd read in the file that she was twenty-eight years old.

"The evidence on the man in the airport seemed to indicate desert or rural. And Tara's security indicated the same. That's what we'll have to stick to, barring further evidence."

Emir scowled. "So far it's the best we have."

"Exactly," she agreed.

He watched as she stood, walked into the hallway and over to a white-marble pillar that was just one of many lining the length of the two-hundred-foot hallway. He knew she wouldn't find any answers there. Only space.

As familiar as he was with all of it, he still, at times, felt the overpowering opulence of the office walls. He'd seen her look of surprise when he'd first brought her into his office. He imagined she thought he'd decorated it to suit his personality rather than realizing what it was: a tribute to the generations that had come before him.

If it were up to him, the office would be simpler, less elegant. The rosewood desk was opulent enough to stand alone. Sitting on a richly vibrant, deep, brown-and-blue Persian rug that covered the majority of the floor made it even more so. And yet neither the opulence of the desk nor the richness of the rug or the elegance of the other accessories fit with the pictures on the office wall. Pictures of his brothers and his sister in various locations—a ski hill, a beach—and at all different ages, and then a picture of all of them together. He knew that it all appeared as if he'd moved into someone else's home and never added anything to his own liking, except, possibly, the pictures. And it didn't matter to him. This was his family's history and he honored it. The decor meant nothing more than that.

He knew she was back, he could sense her before he looked up and saw her. She took a step past the doorway, facing him but not looking at him, obviously focused on her thoughts. He imagined from the expression on her face that she might be replaying in her mind what had been done so far. He waited as minutes passed silently between them before she spoke.

"At least if the tower dump info you requested on the first call would come in…" She walked toward him. "What range are they using?"

"I kept it fairly simple. The city limits and thirty miles out. Fortunately the call came in early in the morning. The traffic was light. There were only a little over six hundred," he said. "With Barb, we've got the best on it. We can't do more."

The tower dump had requested cell phone companies in the area to reveal records of users during a specific time frame. It was an invasion of privacy implemented only at the request of law enforcement and, in situations like this, where Nassar Security had pull and reach.

She frowned at him.

"Sorry, you've never met Barb Alamy."

"Not officially," she agreed. "I'm just curious. Western given name…"

"She's an American who came to Morocco on vacation. Long story short, she's been here over a decade, married a local man. Now she's the office tech guru and has since taken over research."

"I don't know how you found her, but Barb's definitely a tech guru."

"She found us," he admitted of his recent addition. "And now we have her working in both offices."

"She'll be busy on this one."

A minute later she yawned. "We should get some sleep. Or at least try," she said.

She was right. He'd woken this morning into a nightmare and hadn't had time or thought to even run a comb through his hair. His only consideration for the last fourteen hours had been Tara and he knew she would be his purpose until she was home safe. Yet, as he met the blue smoke of Kate's eyes, he felt oddly connected, calm.

Minutes seemed to tick by like hours. She yawned again and stretched out on one of two leather sofas that rested against opposing corners of the sprawling office. He got up and brought a blanket to her, laying it gently over her.

"You should get some sleep, too," she suggested.

But fifteen minutes later he knew she wasn't going to sleep, either. He could hear her turn this way and that. He stood at the window, the thought of sleep an impossibility. He leaned against the ledge. There was nothing for them to do and nowhere for them to go, and it was killing him.

Suddenly her phone buzzed a warning for an incoming text message. He turned around and switched on a nearby light as she sat up, the blanket spilling around her waist, and pulled her phone from her pocket. There was something oddly erotic at seeing her in that state, sleepy, although she hadn't slept, her hair mussed, as if she'd just had a passionate... He bit back the thought.

"I didn't know that you left my number for the tower dump info," she said.

"My phone stays here," he said, his voice husky with conflicting emotion, fear for Tara, desire for Kate. Only one of those emotions was acceptable and it seemed he could control neither. "I'll take the satellite phone."

"I suppose I should have assumed that as we're not taking your phone with us."

"Right. Zafir will be acting in my stead. Pretending to be me."

She paused as she read the message. She frowned. "The location changed slightly. Barb says the original call came from thirty miles southeast of Marrakech." She scrolled down and then looked up.

"We head out at first light exactly as we planned, nothing changes," he said. "Anything else?"

"I'd suggest we leave earlier. We could be going deep into the desert or not." She shrugged. "It's a crap shoot at this point and we don't know what we might encounter. We can make up time on the highway at night, head in the general direction of that call. That way, if anything goes wrong or changes— we're already on the road. I'd feel better about that. I'm sure you would, too."

Minutes passed and turned into an hour. The silence was becoming unbearable.

Then Emir's phone rang and he pulled it from his pocket and looked at the caller ID.

"Faisal."

He was surprised, and yet oddly not, to see that it was his brother. Faisal was the only one in the family who hadn't known about Tara. He guessed that was no longer the case.

"Yeah," he answered, thinking how few telephone conversations he had with Faisal except on a business level. They usually communicated by text. That fact alone told him that Faisal knew what had happened.

"I heard about Tara, man." There was tension and worry straining Faisal's voice.

Emir gripped the phone, wishing he had news, something to give his brother, hope for all of them. Faisal was close to Tara in ways neither he nor the rest of his brothers were. For Zafir and Emir, and even Talib, she had been the child they had raised. For Faisal, who was nearest in age, she was his childhood playmate and friend, and even now, as adults, they were close to each other. That was one of the key reasons why Emir didn't trust Faisal not to go off on a mission to kill those who had taken his sister. As a result, they had delayed telling him.

He'd meant to call in the minutes before he put together what was needed to take him and Kate safely into the desert, but Faisal had beat him to it. "How'd you find out?"

"When were you going to tell me?"

"Soon. I didn't want…"

"I had a right to know."

"I know and I would have…" He stopped. He'd waited too long. But what was done couldn't be undone and justification wouldn't change anything. "Who told you?"

"Talib called."

"Talib," he said, and his voice held little inflection as he fought a red cloud of anger. At another time he would have torn a strip off Talib for going against his wishes. But this was an emotional time for all of them. Faisal needed to be told. Emir had just wanted to ensure that the way Faisal heard wouldn't set him off.

"Where are you?" he asked, afraid to hear the answer, knowing that Faisal could be impulsive when it came to something this serious, especially if it involved Tara. His fist clenched and his temple pounded, and he didn't want to hear the answer. His brother could be on a flight to Morocco for all Emir knew. That was the last thing they needed. Too many people looking and Tara could pay with her life. He turned, startled as a gentle hand touched his arm, and he was looking into blue eyes that reminded him of an azure sea. He took a step back, looked away from her mesmerizing eyes, unsure what to make of Kate's touch, but her intent was clear. Calm down.

"At home." Faisal's voice was strained. "But I'm debating if that's smart, if…"

Relief flooded through him that Faisal hadn't boarded a plane and wasn't halfway across the Atlantic on his way there. Hearing his voice…for a moment it was like Tara was in this room, like everything was right. But that wasn't the case. She was still missing. But Faisal was cooperating, for now. "Stay there. We don't need—"

"Me flying over there." Faisal cut him off. "And killing the creeps who did this and anyone else who stands in my way?" Anger and sarcasm laced his words. "Don't worry. I'm not coming over. Not yet. I know we need calm heads to find them and get Tara back, but once that's done…" His words trailed off.

"We're doing everything necessary—"

"Stop!" Faisal warned. "I know you're on this. Adam's already briefed me. No worries," he said before Emir could add anything to that. "Adam will be kicking butt if I make a move to go over there. But, man, I can't do nothing. At least, I'm having a hard time doing it." He laughed. A dry, humorless sound that seemed to make fun of his words more than anything else. "Can you find her? Will you be enough, you and K.J.?"

"We have to be. We need you in Wyoming," Emir reiterated, knowing it was a fact Faisal was well aware of and, despite what he'd said, probably the one reason he was still there. They'd acquired a number of high-profile cases over the last months and Emir only expected more. And, like Faisal, Talib was also occupied with managing their office here, at least until Tara was found. The only difference was that Talib could still be involved, if necessary, for he could be here on a minute's notice, unlike Faisal. He knew that would be tough for Faisal to take, but it was how it had to be.

"Yeah, I know," he said, an edge to his voice that wasn't normally there. "Damn. I just hope she's not frightened."

Frightened. It was a word that hung thick and dark between them. They'd rather have Tara pissed than frightened, but reality danced and darted unspoken between them.

"We'll find her." Emir felt like he was repeating a phrase he'd committed to in blind faith. But this couldn't end any other way than the way he wanted it to end—with Tara, at home laughing with them and at them, as she always did.

"You're still at the compound?" Faisal asked.

"Yeah," Emir said. "But not for long. I'll fill you in soon. Kate and I—"

"Kate?" Despite the gravity of the situation, there was an amused edge to Faisal's voice that made Emir feel oddly defensive.

"K.J.," he said, shifting to the initials that it

seemed everyone else used, and yet she'd asked him to call her Kate. But it was more than that. To him, she was Kate, not K.J. He shifted the phone from his left ear to his right, as if that would change the fact that his brother had just hinted there might be something in his feelings for Kate that was more than employer and employee. Utterly ridiculous. He liked her. They were partners in this case, nothing else. "We're heading out just before dawn. We're trying to play it low-key, not look like we're doing anything more than waiting."

"So what do you have on them?"

"Not much. We think there might be two groups, unorganized, possibly not working together. We'll track them to the last phone call and from there, after what Ahmed said, we think they might be heading into the Sahara." He hesitated. What they had was so little—nothing to go on. "Zafir will handle negotiating with them going forward." He didn't mention the fiasco at the airport. None of that was relevant, not now, at least not to Faisal, and could only convince him that he was needed. Right now, giving him less information was for the best, as was involving less people.

"Exactly what I would have done," Faisal said shortly, the frustration evident in his voice.

"Look, I'll be in touch." Emir hesitated again. "If you have any…"

"Ideas. Yeah, you bet I'll call. And, by the way,

about K.J.—Kate," he corrected, that infuriating hint of amusement back in his voice. "You might only have known her for a short time, but I believe our father fell for Mother in the space of twenty-four hours." He chuckled at his dig.

"We'll find her," Faisal said, the humor replaced by an edgy determination.

"We will," Emir repeated and clicked off. So far he'd managed to ensure that Faisal was staying put, for now. He sank back in the rich leather chair that had been his father's, put his elbows on the massive desk and lowered his head to his arms.

"Bloody lie," he muttered, for, despite his words, in his heart he was very afraid there was the possibility of failing, of losing Tara. It was a possibility he'd refused to admit but it was a fear that had harbored like a thorny intruder in his heart since the beginning.

Chapter Seven

Kate looked at her watch. "I feel like we should have something substantial to move on but yet if it were like any other case…" Her voice trailed off.

"But it's not," he said. "Especially the way it's been going. They're not following a norm. Two demands for money. You know that's not normal or, at least, standard behavior."

"They're not rushed. They feel like they have time. That's a good thing."

He didn't reply as he stood at the window, the same one he'd stood at all those hours ago after he'd first received the news of Tara and while he'd waited for his brothers. He was pulled to the window, and had been throughout the evening, to the lights of Marrakech that seemed to lead him beyond and to the outside of the city. But there was no promise of answers. All he could see was a memory, Tara's face—smiling, happy. But all that had vanished. Instead she was in jeopardy. He tried to focus on the city, on taking his mind elsewhere and in that way relaxing enough to possibly come up with another angle—an idea that had yet to be considered.

He turned, looked to the right at the lights of the more modern city center and business hub. Then his gaze moved to where the ancient beginnings of Marrakech lay, taking in the labyrinth of tight streets and passageways, where businesses and residences hid behind ancient walls and where tourism and local shopping blended easily with snake charmers and tattoo artists.

The art and culture that crowded the narrow streets came from a heritage they all shared, from beginnings somewhere deep in the heart of the wind and sun-carved desert. It was a place of mystery and charm and one that hid the good as easily as it hid the bad.

His grip tightened on the window ledge. This was doing no good at all. For it was from the country's heart that Tara had been taken.

"Emir? What is it?"

Kate's voice had that caress, subtle, unintentional, but it reached to the heart of who he was, to places he hadn't let anyone in, in a very long time.

He couldn't look at her. He couldn't bear the sympathy he told himself he knew she was feeling. She didn't understand—couldn't—for, no matter how well intentioned, to her, Tara was just a case. She couldn't be anything else, for Kate didn't know her.

They'd never met. "Nothing. Get some sleep while you can."

"I already tried that, didn't work."

He could hear her moving quietly in the darkness. Only the wafting scent of coconut combining oddly with the faint scent of myrrh alerted him that she was near. He didn't know how it had come to be, that the scents of his homeland seemed such a part of her.

And then she was beside him. "It's beautiful even at night."

He said nothing. There was nothing to say.

"She's not just a case," she said as the moments of silence turned into minutes. "Not to me. Not like you think."

He started. How had she read his mind? She lay a hand over his where it rested on the ledge. She'd done that before, but this time heat seemed to run through his core, connecting them in a way he was unable to analyze, wanting him to turn to her to… he pulled his hand away.

He was torn. Worry for Tara, fury at her captors and now the conflicted feelings toward Kate. He had to get it together and that meant focusing on something completely different.

There were hours before they could move into action but, in the meantime, they needed to set safeguards in place. He picked his phone up and turned it over. "It's our only contact with them—the pigs who have Tara." He put the phone down. "I don't like the idea of leaving it...of trusting..."

"Zafir will be fine," Kate assured him. "They'll never know it's not you. And we'll be in touch." She looked at her watch. It was only 7:55 p.m.

"How do you know he won't slip? That—"

"You're not giving him credit."

He shook his head. "Zafir's good, but this is Tara we're talking about. Any one of us could break under the pressure. We—"

"Stop." Her shoulder brushed against his. "I'd work with any of you in a heartbeat. And in a case like this, the most important one you'll ever work, no one's going to mess up." She looked at him and he knew she could see the doubt in his face. He couldn't hide it. He'd never doubted any of their abilities before, but it had never mattered so much.

"Zafir is good," she repeated. "You know that. And I can vouch for him. I've read some of the cases he was involved in." She smiled. "Despite the talk—he's good."

Emir turned to face her. She'd taken the elastic out of her hair and now her long, straight, blond locks hung loose and soft, framing her face and skimming well past her shoulders.

"Interesting, your brother."

"What do you mean?"

"The rumor is that he's always got a romance

going. Most recently a model. Gorgeous redhead."
She laughed.

"Office talk?" He frowned. He abhorred gossip.

"I'm sorry," she murmured. "I was trying to
lighten the mood. Inappropriate, I know..."

He glanced down and saw that she wove her fingers together—long, delicate fingers. Sensitive fingers, Tara might have said, but Tara had always been
an intuitive sort. *Is*, he reminded himself. They'd
find her.

"Emir, listen."

She shifted, her hair gleaming in the gentle, low
light of the reading lamps. Again the delicate scent,
the combination that was so uniquely her, wafted
from her and seemed to overwhelm him, to make
him more aware of her than he wanted or needed
to be.

"I'm listening," he said.

She looked up at him. "I feel like there's something eluding us."

"So let's go over it again—what we know," he
said with relief to be doing something.

She leaned against the desk.

He leaned back against the window ledge. "I don't
know what we could have missed. She was taken by
one, maybe two, men outside the gates, but we know
there were others involved."

"If two of them died this afternoon, how many are

left?" Kate asked as if the attack had been no more traumatic than a trip to the grocery store.

"What are you suggesting?"

"That there are no others." She shrugged. "I know that sounds unrealistic, impossible even, but we have to explore every option."

"That isn't an angle we've even considered."

"There hasn't been a demand in hours. Since the attack…" Her words hung in the silence between them, which seemed dark and treacherous now that the disturbing alternative had been presented.

"I don't think it's possible." The truth was that he didn't want to think it was possible since it brought forth so many other options. But that wasn't who he was; he had to go there—to explore possibilities that were difficult to consider.

"That she's out there in the night…" His voice threatened to break. He took a deep swallow and breathed out the last word, and it almost broke him. "Alone."

He pushed away from the window and began pacing the room. He stopped as he faced the window again, his thoughts focused on the terror of that one thought. It was more horrific than anything that had come before. A shudder ran through him, deep and agonizing. He couldn't imagine his baby sister alone, possibly terrified.

"She's tough," Kate said. "That was clear in everything I've read. And, truly, what I said earlier,

I'm sorry. I've only added more worry by introducing the possibility."

"Don't be." He cut her off, hearing the gravel edge of emotion in his voice.

"I doubt very much if it's true. There'll be another demand. Those men might be a splinter group or part of the main group who wanted you out of the picture for whatever reason, and me, as well. I think both those explanations hold more validity than my other theory."

"We can't discount anything."

"And definitely not the fact that they're going to be demanding more money. Three hundred and fifty thousand, considering what your family is worth, isn't a lot for all the trouble they're going to. They seem to know you won't call the authorities." She cleared her throat. "And having said that, ignore my last hypothesis—that there are no others. It doesn't fly."

"You're right." He took a breath. "But why are they taking their sweet time to demand more?"

"To put you on edge. Which will obviously give them an advantage. You are kept guessing, the stress of waiting, of inertia, wears you down."

He knew she was right about everything but the thought of Tara alone, left in the desert to find her own way out or die. Once that idea had been introduced, he knew it would be almost impossible to dispel.

"I think our original theory that they are a group who, for some reason, started acting against each other is far more plausible," Kate said. "Forget my earlier musings. I was thinking aloud, exploring possibilities."

There was something intuitive about her; a calming presence that put him off balance and made him want to take her in his arms and kiss her.

"Emir?"

He pushed the inappropriate thought from his mind and gave her his full attention.

"It was a theory that probably isn't very plausible. Hopefully we'll have more information, a direction, before we hit the road. If not, we get moving, anyway. With any luck, by this time tomorrow, this will be over—or…" She hesitated. "Or at least close."

Silence hung between them for a minute then two.

"Do you think they meant to keep you from leaving Marrakech and following them?" Kate asked as she mulled over the profiles of the deceased pair of attackers.

"By attempting to kill me or, more appropriately, us?" He could hear the amusement in his voice. If it hadn't been about Tara, he would have enjoyed sparring with her—going over the theories, discounting them, coming up with new ones.

"I don't think they expected me or Dell. And when they realized you weren't alone, it all fell apart." She stood, paced the length of the office.

"So, opening fire at the edge of airport property was to threaten the family."

"Exactly. You were the one who would go after them. They knew that."

"And Faisal or any of the others wouldn't?"

"Faisal is an ocean away. Zafir is more apt to play their game and, of course, Talib will agree with Zafir. He usually does." She smiled. "Not that Talib doesn't have his own mind, but he tends to think much like Zafir." She looked at him. "Whereas you? You will play to a point but it won't stop you from going after her. You're more like Faisal than you know." She smiled. "You're wondering how I know that."

"Am I?"

"I've studied many of the agency's past cases and I've spoken to Adam. I might not be completely right, but I think I'm close. As far as Talib is concerned?" She put a finger to her chin as if considering. "Middle child. I filled in the blanks—classic."

"Assumption," he said with a pained attempt at a smile. "But impressive."

"And you? Oldest child, responsibility of raising a younger sibling foisted on you at a young age. Serious. Determined. In charge. Textbook."

"So this was all about getting me out of the way?" he asked and couldn't kill the sarcasm in his voice. "The theory must seem like overkill, even to you."

"Maybe. Or maybe not," she said. "Think about it."

There were so many different angles in any kidnapping case and because it was Tara, there seemed even more. The silence since the last call they'd received from the kidnappers terrified him, not for himself but for Tara. She was everything and it was up to him to make sure she came back, for their family was nothing without her.

"Emir…" Kate began, her hand reaching for his.

He shook his head. He couldn't remember a time in his life when he'd felt any lower, any more desperate. It was an out-of-control feeling that terrified him and he knew he had to get it together.

He looked at Kate and wished that he hadn't. He couldn't handle the compassion in her beautiful eyes. Her lips were slightly parted and seemed to offer the only chance at hope he had in this dark and dreadful night.

He leaned down and, as his lips met hers, he felt the power of what the two of them were and had proved only a few hours ago. Now he felt a different power, the power of where her soft lips could take him, where the taste of her could lead, where… He drew back, leaving the kiss as only a sweet meeting, a gentle caress, leaving the potential behind.

"I'm…" He wasn't sure what he'd been about to say. His emotions were playing with his logic and all he wanted to do was to kiss her again. He shoved the feeling back. The life-and-death adrenaline rush had awoken another primitive need, nothing more.

But as he turned his back to her and faced the city, the haunting tones of the call to prayer began. The ancient notes pierced the silence and taunted the occupants of that one room in the Al-Nassar compound with the reminder of how life was so much more important than the moments that defined it.

And worse, that time was slipping away.

Chapter Eight

Monday, September 14, 8:15 p.m.

Emir's phone beeped just as the call to prayer ended, as if the solemnity of the one had somehow influenced the other. He pulled the phone out of his pocket as his eyes met Kate's and he knew they were on the same page. She connected with him like no one, no woman, ever had. It was different than how he connected with Zafir, for this connection felt intimate. It was another thought he didn't want to consider. All he wanted to consider right now was that they were back in business.

"Zafir," he said for Kate's benefit. He'd known without looking at his phone, with an instinct that they'd had since birth, that it was his twin. "What do you have?" he asked. He nodded at Kate's look and pressed the speaker button as he alerted his twin, "You're on speaker."

"An ID on one of your attackers. Unfortunately

we couldn't find anything on the other. But the one we did find…well, he's got an interesting trajectory."

Emir looked up and met the full impact of Kate's thoughtful yet intense look. She was leaning forward, her chin in the palm of one hand and her phone in the other. He started when he realized she was recording the call. She was good, proving once again that she was one step ahead of him.

For a minute it was as if neither he nor Kate breathed. It was the news they were looking for, hopefully a lead. Emir gritted his teeth. He was almost afraid to ask but he hadn't succeeded in life by being afraid or by clinging to superstitious silence. "Who is he?" he asked, allowing for only a brief hesitation.

"Atrar Tashfin. Berber—and one would think that's simple enough but there's something a bit strange about him."

Emir choked back an impatient involuntary reaction at what he considered Zafir's theatrics. Short and simple, that's what he lived by and what he preached to his siblings. But he was cut off almost immediately by Zafir's next words.

"Here's the thing. We tagged Atrar. That's the one you thought came out of the Sahara. You know, the one with the fancy boots? The sand and camel dung—"

"Knock-off Ralph Lauren," he interrupted as if that mattered.

"Yeah, it's the same one. He belongs to a Berber village on the south edge of the Atlas Mountains. The village of Kaher. I looked it up and it's pretty remote, backs the mountains but fronts the beginnings of the Sahara. I think you need to pay it a visit. There might be answers there and it's a good place to start. It might be better than what you've been doing. So you can get moving now, rather than waiting, agreed?"

"Agreed," Emir said shortly. "Someone in that village may know something."

Kate's attention was fixed on him but there was a troubled look on her face and he knew she was already going through possibilities. He'd never lacked confidence, but with her beside him, he felt like he could have scaled Everest without equipment. No woman had ever made him feel like that. No woman had needed to, but Kate... He let the thought trail, not sure what it all meant.

"What about the other?" Emir asked, looking over as Kate nodded approval, as if he'd read her mind or, at least, as she'd showed in the short time she'd been here, that she was on the same wavelength.

"Can't get anything on him. Not yet," Zafir replied. "I'm sure the authorities will have an ID eventually, but we can't wait. So I'm giving you what I've got."

"Emir!" Kate whispered urgently.

"Just a minute," Emir said to his twin.

"We need to get there as soon as possible. Does he have the coordinates?" Kate was on her feet.

"I sent them to your email, Em," Zafir said.

"There could be more information there and a more specific area—" She broke off, a worried expression on her face.

"Exactly what I was thinking," Zafir agreed, his voice slightly distant through the speaker phone.

"Is it possible to land anywhere nearby?" Emir asked.

"There's a short landing strip. I've spoken to them and they'll have it lit for you," Zafir said.

"This confirms what we were already thinking." Emir looked at Kate and saw the same urgency he felt, to get going, reflected in her eyes. Already he was planning their new strategy even as he saw the intense look on Kate's face, the frown that marred her normally smooth brow and knew she was considering options. None of his agents did any less than think on their feet. It was how they succeeded in some of their most difficult cases and how they protected the clients they had—how they had become number one on two continents.

"The sooner someone gets there, the better. I'd go there myself..." Zafir paused. "But apparently I'm on Emir duty."

Emir gave a half smile. It was how Zafir had always referred to the times when they had switched roles, more notably in their youth. As adults, this was the first time they'd resorted to such tactics.

"Kate and I have it covered." He looked at her with a wry smile, thinking how much his opinion of her had changed and how, only a few hours ago, he couldn't imagine himself saying that. But she'd more than proved herself in the short time they'd known each other. She'd proved her skill in the best and worst situations. She'd been willing to take a bullet for the cause. Fortunately, good marksmanship on both their parts and Dell's had prevented that from happening.

"We'll fly tonight. Hopefully we can get there soon enough to get some answers. That means you, like you said, lead this show. Tara's kidnappers have to be heading into their final act and asking for more and soon. I don't think they can play this out much longer." He looked over at Kate, who nodded agreement.

"I'm a good twenty minutes away," Zafir replied.

"We'll wait."

"That's not all I've got. I think I have a major lead, man. More than what I just told you, but you needed to know that first. There's no getting around the fact that someone has to go there. And, as we agreed, that's you and K.J.," Zafir said. "But there's something else," he repeated.

"Shoot."

"A sighting—and it's a good chance it might be Tara."

"Why didn't you say that right away?" Emir's eyes met Kate's, his heart pounding at the idea—hope and fear seeming to converge at what this might mean.

"Because I think it's more important you get to the village."

"You thought? Zaf, this isn't your case."

"She's my sister, too. You're not the only one who is torn up about it," his brother growled. "Look, this is what I have. A girl who looks like Tara was reported in Ouarazate Province by a couple of Berbers."

"When?"

"That's the problem. We received the information late. The man who reported it said they'd seen her just before noon today. At the time, they didn't know about the kidnapping. Word's gotten out since then. I think what happened may have been let out by our own staff at the compound. You know, mentioning something of our situation to friends or family. Many of them or their families have ties to the desert. Anyway, he contacted me as soon as he heard. They said they came upon the group over twelve hours ago and they were in a Jeep. There were five of them and the girl."

Emir cursed under his breath. Ouarazate, the gateway to the desert. But too much time had gone by; they could be anywhere.

"Look, I'll be there as soon as I can. There are a few things I have to clear up here and then, depending on the traffic…" Zafir paused, as if considering options. "Don't wait. You've got to get moving. There is too much that needs to be done. Too much at stake."

"You're right. Tara can't wait," Emir said.

"Get moving. Let's get our sister," Zafir said.

"Done," Emir said and clicked off.

TARA CRINGED. She hated the dark, the shadows her imagination had the uncanny ability to turn into more threats than those she already faced. Time seemed to be crawling by and the darkness was never-ending. Without the moon, the night was only broken by the few, too distant stars, and by the fire that crackled and spit over thirty feet away. There was a tent, but she preferred to sit outside it and, oddly, they'd allowed that one request.

Maybe, somewhere in the back of his mind, the leader remembered her for who she was and what she had been to him. Whatever the reason, she was grateful. Somehow it seemed safer here where there was some distance between her and them. She clutched the blanket. It was cold again tonight. She shivered and her eyes never left the fire and the men around it. It wasn't safe for her to take her eyes off them. She'd learned in the early hours of her kidnapping that they were unpredictable.

She was so tired. She couldn't help closing her eyes just for a second. A minute passed and then two before she was snapped awake by angry shouts that echoed through the small, struggling oasis.

Tara drew her knees to her chest, wrapping her arms around them as if that would make her smaller, invisible. Her eyes never left the men. Loud voices meant trouble. This time, as usual, it was the leader. It seemed he didn't like what one of the men had said and now the shouts were followed by something even more deadly. Silence. The moon slipped from behind a cloud and bathed the area in light.

She wished she could disappear but there was nowhere to go. Instead she was trapped by the frightening scene in front of her as the man pulled his rifle from his shoulder and hurled it. She watched as the smaller man, who it was meant for, lunged, missed the catch and stood. The moonlight disappeared again as the gun hit the ground and skipped twice along the battered rug she knew, even in the fickle light of the fire, lay on the desert sand.

Now the gun lay forgotten and their raised voices began to dissolve into shouts and yet another fight. It was a relief, for she knew the fights kept their attention from her.

The leader muttered a string of curses in Arabic before he launched himself into their midst, punching one and grabbing the other and throwing him to the ground. His voice was harsh and, as usual, louder than necessary. She closed her eyes and hoped they remained there—killing themselves in their fight would be ideal. But, as always, she knew this fight wouldn't last long.

She prayed he'd stay away from her. Her prayers went unanswered as minutes passed, silence ensued and then came what she had hoped wouldn't.

She could see him clearly as he approached. His face was highlighted in the moonlight. It was so familiar and yet so very strange. She dropped her gaze, not wanting to meet his eyes, hoping he would leave, change his mind. Instead the sand crunched beneath his heavy boots and he squatted beside her.

She looked up and met the odd yet gentle smile. The smile didn't match the dark look in his eyes. She dropped her gaze to the sand. She could smell the sweat of him, like he hadn't bathed in weeks or even months. He was too near and she fought not to move away for she had nowhere to go and little rope with which to do it.

She drew back, trying to make herself small. He wasn't the man she remembered.

He chuckled as he ran a knuckle along her cheek.

She fought not to cringe or to move away. Although there wasn't far to move; the rope gave her five feet of freedom.

This time she blew out a relieved breath as he stood to join the others.

"Do you know what stands between us and

wealth?" she heard him ask. But it was his reply that made her cringe. "Death."

She shuddered, trying not to think of whose death he might be implying. She watched as the moonlight reflected across his face and clearly showed the disfiguring scar that covered the left side. The scar made a mockery of what had once had been a handsome face. Close up, she knew the scar appeared raw, almost painful, despite the fact that it was clear it had been from wounds long healed.

But it was then that she heard the most frightening thing of all. His promise to take down the house of Al-Nassar, to take what it held most precious and to leave nothing to remind anyone it had ever existed.

Chapter Nine

"Kaher is on the fringe of the Sahara, like Zafir said. Not well used by tourists and hikers, but that might be to our benefit." Even Kate could hear the trace of excitement in her voice. "What incredible luck that they have an airstrip."

She ran her fingers through her hair and looked at him. His dark eyes were both grim and determined. "That information certainly came out of nowhere," she added. "Let's hope someone knew this guy. Like, who he was hanging with, what he was doing…"

"And we can find out who and what they know quickly," Emir said.

"At least before first light," she agreed, grimacing. "You've flown at night? I mean, you have experience at this sort of thing?"

"You doubt me?"

"No." She shook her head. "Of course not. I was just surprised."

"I'm a qualified pilot and I've flown at night

often," he assured her. "I'll get us there in one piece, if that's what you're worried about."

"Did I say I was worried?" She cocked an eyebrow at him. "Let's get moving."

But before either of them could act on those words, her phone dinged, signaling a text message. She looked at it with a frown then back up at him. "It's a blocked text—no identification." She held up her index finger, warning him to silence. "This is odd."

Outside, a siren broke the quiet; the distant sound knifing in through an open window. The flashing lights seemed to pulse through the night, as if forewarning them of something even more threatening than what they already faced.

Seconds seemed to tick away and the silence within the room wrapped around them in a thick, almost choking veil.

Her eyes met his and she pushed a button on the phone.

"It's a video."

She looked up, saw the perspiration dotting his forehead and wondered if the pressure of it all was finally getting to him. She dismissed the thought. He was strong, too strong. There were other words for men such as him… Just his nearness could take a woman's breath away. She'd bet that he'd never had a woman turn him down. She remembered how, earlier, he had been outlined in his office by the city lights as he'd stood by the window, how his well-muscled form had been clearly defined by his T-shirt.

She was always in control and now, at a completely inappropriate time, her mind was running amuck thinking of...

She frowned and clutched the phone tighter. "It might be nothing—"

"Or it might be from them," he said, cutting her off.

And they both knew what he meant. Tara's kidnappers.

Her finger lifted from the phone as if that were a deal-breaker. "Maybe I should watch it without you."

"No, start it. We need to see it and see it now."

They didn't know what was on the video. It could be anything or anyone. But in this situation, with everything that had happened, the possibility that it wasn't a ransom demand in some form, that Tara wasn't involved, was slight.

"Start it," he said thickly as he leaned over her shoulder.

They watched the video begin with no prelude but, rather immediately, a woman's face dominated the screen.

"Tara," he said, an edge to his voice.

Her hands were tied and she was kneeling, looking right at them or, more aptly, at the camera or at whoever was filming her.

"Please, Emir," Tara said, her voice pleading. But

the words didn't seem as panicked as they seemed forced. It was as if she wasn't saying them voluntarily but instead was being coached. She hesitated and stumbled over what she was saying, sounding reluctant.

Kate swallowed. It was tough to watch. There was a flashlight on her face and Tara blinked frequently, squinting against the light. Her dark hair was long and loose, curling wildly around her dusty face. Her faded jeans were torn, not as a fashion statement, Kate suspected, but more a result of her ordeal. Her flowered, peasant-style cotton blouse had chalk-colored streaks running through it. There were numerous thin, red scratches on her hands and across one cheek, but she met the camera with fire in her eyes despite the tears on her cheeks.

"Tara," Emir murmured. "Hang in there. I'm coming."

In the video, Tara turned slightly, as if she might have heard him.

She sat on her heels on what looked like a burgundy blanket, but it was faded with age and dusty with sand. It was hard to tell if the blanket might have some sort of ethnic origin, a clue to who she was with or where she was, but that clue was lost as the camera never went near enough to give them a clear visual.

Kate tried to remain objective as she watched an animated, if you could call it that, Tara. This was the first time she'd seen her in anything other than a still photo. She made a mental note of her mannerisms and listened to what she said as she looked for signs of coaching and for some hint of who was with her. She was fairly sure that she had a better chance of seeing any of that than Emir, who was too close to be objective.

Kate looked at Emir, who confirmed everything she had thought, as anger seemed to emanate from him in the tightness in his lips and the intense way he looked at her. She knew that any objectivity he had maintained had been lost in the moment. It wasn't surprising. Anyone in his situation would have reacted the same, although in her mind he was holding on better than most. Still, objectivity and her skill in these situations, was why she was here. But now she feared that the deeper they got into this, the closer they got to finding Tara, the more difficult it would be for Emir to keep a check on his emotion. She didn't blame him, it was natural, but she also knew it wasn't going to help the investigation one bit.

"They want it in American dollars." There was no emotion in Tara's voice.

The video blurred and garbled and then became clear again.

"Someone will tell you when and where," Tara said, her words a monotone, as if she were reading a script.

There was a sound behind her, a scuffling, and

then the video blanked out and came back on. This time Tara was gone and the muffled voice of a man was saying, "Be prepared, you'll have little time."

The video clicked off.

"What kind of joke is this?" Emir stormed. "They prop her up, ask for money yet again, and don't give a drop zone, an amount, even a time—nothing?"

Kate looked at him, at the fire in his dark eyes and the pain that overrode everything, and couldn't begin to imagine how it might feel. Even if she'd had siblings, she doubted she could imagine such a nightmare. She wished she could fix it, that it wouldn't carry on any longer. That somehow she could end it.

"So they want what they asked for earlier or it's another amount. Whatever it is, will that be enough? Will they let her go?" Emir's voice was raised and tense.

Kate didn't say anything. This was about Emir regaining control. He didn't need or want anything from her right now.

Silence flooded the room.

"Get in touch with Zafir. Now," she said after a minute had passed.

She listened to the one-sided conversation as Emir laid out what had happened and what Zafir needed to do.

He put the phone down and ran splayed fingers through his hair before he looked at her. "He's already on the way."

"Let's watch that video again. Can you? Is it too much…?"

"Start it," he rasped.

They watched it through two more times before she turned it off and set the phone down.

"She was in the open. There wasn't any shelter." His words were like grim drumbeats of doom.

"Emir," she warned as she shook her head, "don't go there. None of that is relevant, not now. She's not comfortable but she's not injured and she's not—" She bit off the last words.

"Dead." He filled the word in for her. "And she's not going to be, either." He looked at his watch. "Where the hell is Zafir? It's been…"

"Two minutes," she noted. "Look, let's review that video one more time. There was something I wanted to mention but I thought it was a nervous tic, considering what was going on. Where she was, what—"

"Tell me," he broke in.

She looked at him, saw the pain in his eyes that he was struggling to contain and her heart almost broke. He was a strong man but even strong men had their limits.

"I think she's trying to tell us something."

She picked up the phone and pushed Play. The video no sooner began to run before she hit Pause. "Did you see that slight tapping of her finger on her left hand?"

He frowned. He leaned closer. "Son of a desert stray," he muttered.

He hit Rewind again and again.

"This is difficult," she said, thinking how hard it was to watch his sister being held captive like that—to see she wasn't alone but surrounded by her captors. That much was evident based on the fact they could see the boots of two men obviously milling nearby. They were boots that, this time, gave them no clue. They were clean, generic, with no sign of sand or dirt—no evidence of any kind.

Kate turned her attention back to Tara. When she'd first noticed the thumb tapping on Tara's left hand, she had thought it might be anxiety. The woman had much to be anxious about.

"I don't believe it," Emir said. "Why didn't I see that before? Morse code."

"Interesting," Kate said as she thought of the eclectic collection of books on Tara's shelves and looked closer at the video.

Emir said nothing but his presence seemed to fill the room even as his attention was on the video.

"Simplistic and yet—" Kate broke off. Tara was surprising her in ways she hadn't expected. Morse code was not something a young woman of Tara's generation would have any exposure to. "Or would she?" she asked softly.

Emir turned. There was a troubled frown on his

face as he watched her, his eyes seeming to lock with hers. "What are you thinking?"

"The implausibility of this…" She remembered the bookshelf. Tara wasn't just a modern girl with an attitude, she was also a serious student and an avid reader. The books on her shelves had been everything from contemporary novels to history. But one shelf had stood out. The section filled with procedural books and one, she remembered, labeled, "Code This."

"She studied Morse code?"

Emir nodded. "Not so much studied as read some books she'd found in what had been our father's private library. Like I said, it was nothing serious— goofing around, she called it. She was only fourteen or fifteen. Back then we often practiced it together in English and French. I didn't think she remembered."

Kate looked at the video. Now she watched the subtle, yet clear when you noticed it, up-and-down movement of Tara's thumb. Because her hand was a bit behind her, it wasn't something that caught your eye, or, she suspected, the eye of the cameraman. She narrowed her eyes, watching the furtive movements, the rhythm and the pattern in the long and short gestures.

Around Tara were the canvas walls of what seemed to be a tent but the video was edited enough that what was around her wasn't clear. It could be a tent anywhere or, from what Kate could see, it could not be a tent at all. But one thing was now clear. She looked closer, but once she'd made the determination, the truth was inescapable.

Emir's attention was solely on the video. Kate frowned at the thought of the obsolete code in a time when even cursive writing was almost extinct. But there was no denying that Tara was definitely trying to tell them something. The video cut off just as her thumb lifted again.

Emir looked at Kate with a frown ridging his brows. He rubbed the back of his hand across his cheek. "T-e-n e-t-e," he said, spelling it out. "It makes no sense." He ran the video again, as if going through the series of taps would change anything. The video cut off again before any more information could be divulged and before Tara's kidnappers could see what she had done. "And there's nothing more."

The room felt suddenly close, as if there were no oxygen. Kate could feel the energy of the man beside her as the tension and fear for his sister seemed to pulse between them and something else.

"Été," he said. "French for 'summer.' What summer? Where?"

"Ten," she murmured, moving what he'd just said to memory for later consideration. "Could refer to anything, but my best guess is that it refers to something about her."

"She wasn't finished. She thought she had more time. That's why it was cut off the way it was."

"Possibly."

Kate was quiet, thinking of what it all might mean. When she met his eyes she saw the silent strength and the determination in his chiseled jaw and, for a moment, it was like she forgot to breathe.

"Do you remember she gave a victory sign at the beginning?"

He frowned. "She used to do that as a kid on the first day of summer vacation or on the announcement of a family trip."

There was silence for a moment before he spoke.

"Ten," he repeated just as she had earlier. "Could she have mixed English and French? Tara is fluent in both. She's stressed. She could have used the languages interchangeably."

"Go on," Kate encouraged.

"The year Tara was ten, the most notable thing was that that was the summer my parents took her and Faisal for a short tour of the Sahara." He stood. "Could it be that easy?"

"She wouldn't want to make it difficult, yet she didn't know how much time she'd have. Thus the cut-off words." She looked at him. Saw the hope in his eyes.

A thought came to her that, somehow, what Tara's security, now so critically wounded, and what Tara had just tried to tell them were connected. "Could what Ahmed have been trying to tell you also have been a place?" She looked at him. "Emir? Where in the Sahara did your parents take Tara that summer? What was their final destination?"

"El Dewar." He smacked his hand on the desktop. "I'd forgotten about it. I don't know how I could have."

"It was trivial detail at the time, especially since you weren't involved in the trip," Kate said. "Understandable."

"That was the farthest they went before returning home. But is that the clue?"

He was quiet for a minute, considering what she had said. "Davar. Could Ahmed been trying to name the place and now she's trying to tell us the same? That she's near El Dewar, or there's information to be had at El Dewar, the same Berber village she saw at ten?"

"It's a possibility but it's also a big stretch," Kate said. She grabbed the map. "It's a small place. I doubt if she's there now. She couldn't be hidden and there are enough people that not everyone would be complicit. So, could she be near there? Is that possible?"

He didn't answer. Instead his fists were clenched, his lips in a straight line, his mind obviously elsewhere. Fighting, she imagined, with long-forgotten memories.

"Emir!" Her voice was sharp. It was the only way to get through to him. He was ready to hit the desert without a plan, with only guns and rage, and neither of those would be successful in rescuing his sister.

He looked at Kate as if seeing her for the first time. "I'm sorry. I lost it, I shouldn't have…" He paused, as if he needed time to breathe. "You have no idea," he said.

Time seemed to beat slowly between them and, for a second, all she could do was look at the strong jaw, feel his solid presence, and wish that was all it took—a minute in his arms to make all of this right for him. She shoved the thought away.

"You're right, I don't. But what I do know is that my decisions aren't clouded by emotion. Yours are." She took his hand in both of hers and tried not to acknowledge the irony of her words. "Listen to me." She looked at him. His rich dark eyes were pools of pain. "That's what the kidnappers want, for you to irrationally follow their demands without thought. That was more than likely part of the purpose behind that video. Maybe…" she began, thinking of the lack of ransom detail. "All of it. You falling for that ploy won't help Tara. But it might ensure that, if their plan was to kill you at the airport, that scenario will still play out. Only this time, someplace else. You've got to let me lead and help you keep a cool head. It's the only way."

This time when she met Emir's eyes, she saw that, for once, they were dark with hope rather than despair. And something else, as if he were looking at her for the first time. She looked away.

She let go of his hand as he nodded and turned

away from her. The tension seemed to noticeably lift from the room as she blew out a quiet sigh of relief.

"I'm puzzled. Why did they send the video to me?" Kate murmured. "How did they know about me?"

"They've got some sort of inside information. Or maybe they contacted the others when they saw you at the airport."

"How did they find out my name?"

"I don't know," he said, looking at her in a way that had nothing to do with what she was saying.

She was unprepared when he bent and kissed her, and even more so for her own reaction, for the need and want that made her put her arms around his neck and, for a few seconds, to allow herself to sink into that kiss.

It was instinctive and so very wrong. She pushed him back, her hands on his shoulders, creating a distance between them. They were trapped in an emotional situation and it was a natural human reaction to turn from trauma to passion.

He stood there for a moment then his eyes met hers and a truth seemed to pass between them. That what had happened was real, as real as the tragedy unfolding around them. But now it was Tara who eclipsed all and they both knew it.

"She'll die if we don't get her out of there soon," he said. "Let's move."

Chapter Ten

They took off in Emir's Cessna from a runway at the back of the property that wasn't visible from the main entrance. The plane had already been loaded by staff with the supplies they'd need, and Emir had arranged for a Jeep they could use to take them from the village of Kaher into the Sahara.

Now, inside the plane's darkened cabin, they were each immersed in their own thoughts. The roar of the engine and the endless night sky seemed to wrap around them and was only broken by the occasional lights of communities and vehicles traveling on high-ways beneath them.

The golden blanket of lights that had been Mar-rakech was far behind them. Ahead, the shadowed peaks of the Atlas Mountains punctured the night sky and seemed to challenge them to enter. The steady noise of the engine was all that broke the si-lence in the cockpit.

Kate looked to the right, where the dark outline

of the wing seemed almost alien, threatening. She shivered. The darkness sheltered many secrets.

She glanced at Emir, saw the tight grip he had on the wheel and the set of his jaw. She looked at the map in her lap. They'd dropped technology when they'd made the decision to fly to the edge of the desert. Cell towers weren't the norm as one ventured deeper into a place that in some ways was not only off the grid but on another planet. They were also a means of tracking and that went both ways. After Kaher, they were going in electronically silent with no one able to follow their tracks, at least not easily.

Her thoughts shifted and she thought of the northern reaches of the Sahara as it penetrated Morocco. The settlements were mapped in her mind for it was there they'd determined as the most likely area the kidnappers had gone. Now they just needed something a little more specific. She glanced at Emir. She'd been aware of him the entire time the plane had been in the air and all the while she'd studied the map.

"You're all right?" he asked as he turned to her. "You've spent a lot of time studying that map."

"I did. It's calming." She didn't look at him. Even in the dark, she only saw his full lips, felt the memory of them on hers and… She couldn't think of that. It was over, a mistake.

Still, she was relieved to say even those few words for there had been silence for much of the first part of the flight. She'd rather he had spoken. The silence seemed filled with the memory of the brief intimacy they had shared.

None of that had promised anything, she told herself. She looked out the window into the night sky, saw the darkened wisps of clouds and the bulk of the mountains. She pulled her gaze away from the uncertainness of the night sky that was so like her feelings for Emir.

Emir.

She wanted none of his kisses and yet, if she were truthful, she wanted the little she'd received and more. She looked at the map, pulling her attention from the line of his jaw, his strong yet artistic hands on the wheel—imagining how they would feel...

"I've located every community within a hundred miles of Kaher, as well as between that and El Dewar," she said as she pushed her unwanted thoughts away.

"And if they've taken her farther?" There was a rough edge in the timbre of his voice. He looked at his instrument panel and adjusted something, she couldn't say what. Flying in a small plane in the co-pilot seat was not something she did often and never at night.

"The desert won't be easy," Emir said as if another reminder would somehow ease the journey. "I don't know how long it will take to find her. We may need to set up camp—overnight."

It wasn't optimism she heard so much in his voice as something else. There was something almost suggestive in the words, and a shiver ran through her. Alone in the desert with Emir, under different circumstances... She let the thought trail off. Any attraction they felt meant nothing. Danger often got emotions flaring and that led, given the opportunity, to other things. That's all their attraction meant. She should have known better.

"It's impossible to know," Kate agreed, ignoring any connotation an overnight trip might have meant or if there had been any connotation at all. "Hopefully we don't have to enter blind." But that was the point of this trip—to get more information, to be able to enter the Sahara with something more than that Tara's message was connected to a childhood trip. Too bad Tara had been cut off.

Emir glanced at her, his jaw tight, his eyes shadowed in the darkness, and yet she could imagine they were hot and full of passion, a different kind of passion. She believed it was more about finding his sister. None of that was her imagination. His raw emotion filled the cabin with an intensity that caused a shiver to snake down her spine.

Kate knew there was no outcome that was even conceivable to him other than success. All she could do was provide support, be part of the team that pulled Tara out. She reached instinctively for her handgun and felt some comfort at the bulk at her waist. But her hand shook slightly as she realized her feelings had changed. She was no longer there just to get Tara out. She was deluding herself if she thought there was nothing more to this, especially when being in his arms had felt so right.

A tick in Emir's jaw was the only sign of the tension he was under. He flew the small plane with ease, as though flying over treacherous mountains through the dark that seemed to mock them was nothing. She clutched her seat belt and watched for lights, for some sort of indication of civilization, but since they'd entered the mountain range there was nothing. She knew this area of the Atlas Mountains was sparsely settled, mostly by Berber tribes, and that all were remote and distant from each other, including their destination: the village of Kaher.

Kate's phone beeped and she looked at it, startled. "It's a text from Zafir. He wants me to call him," she said even as she punched in the number. They'd kept her phone and planned to drop it at Kaher as the mobile coverage was limited in the Sahara. To lighten what they carried and to limit the possibility of being tracked, they would take only a satellite phone.

The plane dipped slightly to the right as she gripped her seat belt with one hand.

"You're on speaker," she said.

"I didn't know if I'd catch you—" Zafir began.

"What do you have?" Emir interrupted. "We're close to landing."

"I just came from the hospital. Ahmed didn't make it."

"Bloody—" Emir broke off as he slapped his open palm against the wheel of the plane. He reached over and took Kate's free hand, squeezing it. His hand was large and warm, and she felt safe.

"It was tough. His family was there. His wife's pretty torn up."

"Make sure they have what they need," Emir said. "Funeral arrangements…and we'll talk monetary assistance later. Money is the last thing his wife needs to consider, ever."

"The usual, retirement settlement, insurance…we can't bring him back, but she'll be very comfortable."

Kate glanced at Emir, not realizing, or, she supposed, not having a need to know just how much support was available for the families of not only the home compound's employees but agents, as well. She was impressed by both their compassion and their generosity.

"He said something else before he passed," Zafir continued, breaking into her thoughts. "Ajeddig."

"A name, but who?" Emir asked.

Kate frowned.

"It's not much, I know," Zafir said. "That's it, Emir. I'll use the satellite next time. I assume you're ditching the cell."

"Turning it off after this call and dumping it at Kaher," Emir confirmed.

He looked over at Kate, who had opened the map and was running her finger over it.

"Another place name?" she muttered.

"Any luck?" Zafir chimed in as Emir looked at her with a question in his eyes.

"Nothing in Morocco by that name. So, if it's not a place name, what is it?"

"It's got no relevance, at least none that I can find that correlates to anything involving the case," Zafir said. "I'm at the compound now. Got your phone in my hand. I drove in the gate just as you were taking off. That's it, all I've got."

"Thanks, man. I'll touch base as soon as I can."

Kate clicked off just as a strand of lights appeared below. "I thought there was no electricity?"

"In Kaher, no. There's some solar power that's generated and used in parts of the village…the landing strip and a few other buildings. Nothing more."

As he arced the plane she found herself looking straight down at the ground for a few slightly disconcerting seconds and gripped the edge of the seat as if that would somehow prevent the plane from sliding into the abyss beneath them.

The plane leveled off and, as it descended, Kate could see shadowed buildings that seemed to rise from the ground. It was strange, for they weren't skyscrapers or even remotely tall. Instead they were short and squat and crowded into a small space where the mountains ended and the desert began. As she watched, the buildings disappeared as the plane broke through the low-lying cloud cover.

"I've spoken to one of the leaders in the community. A man by the name of Yuften M'Hidi. He'll meet us," Emir said easily as if landing in the dark on the edge of a mountain range was something he did every day.

She laughed. "His parents must have been optimistic. Really? His name means 'the chosen'?"

He smiled as he looked at her. "Firstborn son. It's all about expectations, my dear," he said in a bad imitation of a Southern accent. And he reached over and took her hand and squeezed it.

"Not funny," she said with a smile. But it was a relief to have even a brief moment of levity. They both knew from experience that it did wonders to keep an agent fresh when, as they always did, a case got intense and became a marathon of tension.

The lights on the ground were now clear and the runway stretched beneath them.

"One other thing. We'll be staying tonight at his house. He says he has extra mats for guests. Hopefully, it won't be too grim."

"We aren't expecting luxury," she replied. "If we can get some information, even better. A few hours of sleep would just be gravy," she said with a smile.

"We're going in," he said, still holding her hand as if he knew, despite her silence, how uncomfortable flying in the night in a small plane made her.

She'd never said, but she wasn't letting go of his hand, either. After that there was only the roar of the engine, the dark heaviness of the mountains as they seemed to close in, and the small river of lights that acted as landing lights.

"Despite how I first reacted when I picked you up at the airport," Emir said glancing at her as the plane rolled to a stop, "I couldn't have a calmer, more analytical thinker by my side."

Kate's hand dropped from the seat belt she'd been clutching as the plane rolled along the narrow runway, startled by the unexpected compliment. "Thank you," she said softly.

"More beautiful, either," he added as he brought the plane to a stop.

She wasn't sure if he'd really said that or if she'd just imagined it, rather like the earlier kiss. None of it seemed like the in-charge man she knew, and yet, if she were to profile him…she wouldn't. Instead she enjoyed the instinctive rush of pleasure the compliment gave her and, just as quickly, pulled her mind back to reality. There was no time for such thoughts. Instead, there was silence as they quickly disembarked.

A slight, dark-haired man, whose gray hair glinted in the lights, waved to them as he hurried down the runway.

"Right on time," he said in heavily accented English.

"You've been waiting?" Emir asked.

The words, spoken in Berber, reminded Kate of what she had read about Emir. She knew Berber was a language he had learned as a boy. His father had ensured that he and his siblings were fluent in each of the languages of Morocco. As a result, Emir spoke Arabic, Berber, English and French. The English, he spoke flawlessly, with a hint of American colloquialism. She knew, too, that he'd gone to university in Wyoming where he'd been into all things American. Adam had told her that, along with the fact that Emir was comfortable straddling the Moroccan and American cultures, easily diving into one or the other and enjoying both depending on which country he was in. What nothing had told her was that he was a man she could not only admire but desire in a situation when all of that information was completely inappropriate.

"Good to meet you." Emir reached out a hand to Yuften, who took it with hesitation. Kate guessed the ritual was foreign to the smaller man.

Yuften took a step back, his hands linked behind the back of his navy blue windbreaker. He didn't look at Kate.

She took a step forward, ahead of Emir.

"Kate," she said and didn't offer her hand, knowing it would be an affront to what he believed.

He nodded and turned almost immediately as

Emir took her hand and squeezed it before letting her go.

Yuften spoke, his back to them. "Follow me. My wife will show you where your sleeping mats are later. In the meantime, I believe you have questions," he said in English and in the precise tones of someone unused to using the language. He began to walk away, leaving them to follow as his jacket and matching blue, baggy pants flapped in the light breeze and he almost immediately seemed to fade into the night.

"I'm glad you made it when you did."

They could hear his voice but now he was only an outline in the darkness.

Kate looked at Emir. "What does he mean?" she whispered.

Before Emir could reply, their host answered the question for her.

"Their type isn't welcome here. Killers and the lot."

Time seemed to stand still and only one word echoed between them.

Killers.

Kate shook her head as she looked at Emir.

His hand went to his gun. "Whoever is responsible will die," he said through gritted teeth.

And she knew without question he spoke of Tara's kidnappers and that it was a promise he planned to keep.

Chapter Eleven

Five minutes later, as Emir and Kate followed their host, they found themselves climbing three sets of rough-hewn stairs that were surface-smooth and worn, and made more treacherous by the darkness. The steps ran between small box-like houses that looked very similar. Light, flickering from the entranceways of houses that seemed to close in on them, appeared to come from a candle or kerosene lantern, for it only faintly illuminated patches of the path.

To their left, an older man in a desert-sand-colored *aselham*, also called a djellaba, and the traditional, Berber, long-sleeved robe, led a donkey through a narrow alleyway that wound amid the squat houses and looked to go upward into the foothills and beyond.

It was pushing close to eleven o'clock and the hours before daylight stretched in front of them. The path became more narrow and steep. They navigated another set of primitive stairs as they moved higher, the darkness seeming to deepen and her breath catching as if it had become difficult to breathe. They stopped in front of one house. It was a sandstone-colored building, squat like the rest they'd passed in the last few minutes.

"Here," Yuften said as he stepped through the arched doorway. He motioned with a flick of his right hand that they should follow. Inside, the room was small with soft blue plastered walls and an arched ceiling that made the area feel slightly less cramped.

Three children stared at them. They sat shoulder-to-shoulder, their legs stretched out and their backs pressed to the wall. Kate doubted if the oldest could have been more than six. She guessed that they had been commanded to sit there, for it seemed too formal for a child. She also guessed that only the excitement of strangers visiting had them up this late.

A woman stood quietly just to the right of the doorway. Her hair was covered by a pink, embroidered veil that matched the gray and pink of her traditional robe. A strand of dark hair escaped the veil and her hands were clasped in front of her as she smiled, not looking at anyone but Yuften.

Yuften nodded to her, turned to Emir and said, "My wife, Saffiya." Then he gestured with a sweep of his arm to a solid mahogany table with stubby legs that raised it only a few feet off the floor. He took a place on one side, sitting on a thick emerald-green rug that covered much of the floor. It was clear that they were to follow.

In the corner Kate could see just one chair, a rocking chair, painted orange. She wondered how that cultural anomaly had come to be or how the clash of colors seemed vibrant rather than odd. She turned her attention quickly away, for none of that had any relevance to what they needed to know now. What they needed was information that would bring them to Tara before it was too late.

"You had questions," Yuften said, again in English.

Before they could answer, Saffiya entered the room with a silver teapot and poured them each a cup of tea.

The children giggled.

Yuften raised a hand in a flagging movement without turning around and the children were silent. On a ledge on either side of one wall, a trio of thick candles flickered, throwing shadows across the room.

"Atrar Tashfin—the man you asked about." Yuften looked at them. "He was killed at the Marrakech airport? I can't believe one of ours could be involved." He shook his head. "Of course, he'd been gone a long time, but his father..." He put his teacup down. "How did it happen?"

"A gunfight with the authorities," Emir said.

The explanation was a bit of a stretch, but they were here to get information not give it.

Yuften shook his head, a frown worrying his brow. "It's too bad." He looked at Emir. "Unless he was involved in your sister's kidnapping. Then he had it coming."

"Did you know him?" Emir asked.

Yuften shook his head. "He was here not quite yesterday. But I'd heard he'd gotten mixed up with others. Like I said earlier, thieves and murders." He shook his head. "It's all the same. One leads to the other."

Kate frowned at that as Yuften continued.

"We didn't talk long. But I have heard everything from the others he spoke to. He wanted nothing but money that we didn't have. He stole from me and others…"

"How much?" Emir asked.

"Whatever we could give, but I doubt if he got much." He shrugged. "No one is well off." When he told them the amount that had been stolen from his home, he was right. It was equal to about twenty American dollars.

Their host touched Saffiya's arm. She had sat beside him after the tea was poured. A silent exchange seemed to run between them and then Saffiya nodded and smiled. "Saffiya didn't like him," Yuften said with a nod to her.

He turned back to them. "He'd been away for a

long time. Left for work before he was twenty and, when he returned, his parents were old and had died years before. He never came for their burials but he came now—for money." Yuften shrugged. "He was angry, especially after he'd been here for a few days. My boy said he shoved him aside when he ran too near. A few days ago, when he did leave, he wasn't alone. Four men arrived one day by Jeep— harassed some of our young girls—I had to step in. A few hours later I was glad to see they took him away with them."

Kate glanced at Emir. "Five," she murmured. That could mean there were only three left. Three men holding Tara. But, then again, it was only a guess.

Emir turned his attention to Yuften, who was now looking at his wife. Her lips were pinched.

"Saffiya thinks I should mind my own business. But…" Yuften hesitated. "You have come for information and I have promised you that."

Saffiya shook her head, as if contradicting him, and leaned over to whisper something to him.

"She says that it could be one of our daughters, and that is true. Despite being Berber, he and the others are up to no good. There were rumors later that some of them had killed. Who or what, I don't know. But I fear for the girl."

"What are you saying?" Kate leaned forward, her shoulder brushing Emir's and heat seemed to radiate between them as neither moved, neither pulled away.

"They had a woman with them. Her head and face were covered by a veil."

He stopped and no one said anything, for a veil was not unusual.

"I didn't get close but she didn't seem to belong with them. Her clothes were different. She wasn't one of us. She—" he said with a nod over his shoulder to Saffiya who, despite having stood, hovered by his side, as if to ensure that everything he said met with her approval "—has an eye for clothes. 'City clothes' she called them."

It was clear that while Yuften was acting as if he was in charge of the household, Saffiya was the silent voice of command in this house. She nodded, her eyes gleaming with approval.

Kate leaned forward, her attention on their host. "How did they act toward her?"

Yuften frowned. "I don't know what you mean." He turned to Emir. "They left almost immediately. I didn't have a good feeling about it, but there was nothing illegal, nothing…"

"Did the woman with them seem upset or distressed?" Kate asked.

Yuften shook his head and was about to speak when Saffiya interrupted him.

"This. Here." Her English was fractured and unsure. "She said nothing but…" Saffiya pulled a colorful, beaded bracelet from her pocket. The bracelet was thin, the beads small, a combination of yellow, emerald-green and red, delicate and obviously old. "She dropped." She whispered something to Yuften, who nodded.

"The woman tossed the bracelet to her."

The expression on Emir's face would have frightened Kate if she hadn't come to know him in the intense hours they'd been together. His lips were tight and his dark eyes seemed to gleam with anger.

Yuften's wife nodded as she clasped her hands and moved closer to him.

"It belonged to Tara," Emir said, his lips tightening and his dark eyes pools of pain as he sat still for a minute. No one spoke. Finally he reached to take the bracelet. "She's worn that bracelet since the day she received it. It was our mother's and Tara took it after she died. It was small enough, the strand of beads, to go with any other piece of jewelry. She never took it off. I normally wouldn't remember such a thing but Tara spoke of it often. She always said how it reminded her of Mother. It was as if in doing so she was making sure not just we, but she, never forgot." He shook his head. "As if I ever could."

"Do you know what direction they went?" Kate stepped in, purposely changing the subject as she sensed that what Emir had just heard and then revealed had been emotionally overwhelming.

"South. I heard one of them mention Ajeddig as a place they were going to. They did not know I was close," Yuften said.

Saffiya nodded.

"It means nothing to me. I know no one and nothing of that name." He shrugged. "Flower. What is that?"

A place name again was the first thought that ran through Kate's mind for the word was the same one that Tara's guard, Ahmed, had spoken the last time he'd been able to reveal anything. And yet the map in the plane had revealed nothing. She needed to look at it again. There had to have been something she missed.

"We need the map," she said.

"Come—" Saffiya gestured "—we have books."

Kate followed her as she moved into a smaller room behind the cooking area. Her slim hands lifted the edge of her traditional robe that flowed elegantly around her but threatened to dust the rough cobbles as she walked. Her yellow flip-flops snapped against the stone floor, seeming to keep time as she led Kate up a number of stairs at the back of the room and into another small room. This room seemed to be apart from the rest of the house and held two shelves, each filled with rows of books.

Kate looked around. She hadn't been expecting this. Of the few Berber homes she'd visited, none had had a room dedicated to books. But then, none had been as isolated as this. And even though there were only two shelves that were half the length of the wall they were attached to, it was still unique. In one corner was a wooden school desk similar to any that might be seen in a grade-school classroom in early twentieth-century America. On top of the desk was a metal can full of pens and pencils.

"You teach your children?"

Saffiya nodded with a smile and then pointed to the shelf. "Map," she said as she pulled out an over-size book with no dust jacket and a faded red cover.

"Thank you." Kate took the atlas but continued to scan the shelf. Like the atlas, the remaining books were mainly dust-jacket free with faded red and brown covers, each with a film of dust, despite the claims of homeschooling.

Saffiya backed up then turned and went out the door.

Kate glanced over the titles and realized that the majority of the books weren't in English and that the few that were, were history books. As she took a step back, she instinctively felt like she was no longer alone. She turned to see Emir regarding her solemnly from the doorway.

"Old schoolbooks will get us nowhere," he said.

"I'm not so sure," she said.

She opened the atlas, hoping she could find something, that the promise of a direction would somehow ease his worry, and knowing that nothing short of finding his sister ever could.

"Nineteen-oh-one," she murmured. She flipped the pages slowly and then stopped. "Africa." She walked over to the desk, where she put the open atlas down. She gingerly turned a page, exposing another seemingly frail, yellowed page to the flickering light of the candle Saffiya had left for her.

"Kate, the light is bad, the book is old, there's nothing."

Emir's hands were on her shoulders as he turned her around. She held back a shiver of pleasure as his touch evoked a memory of the earlier kiss and the truth that she wanted so much more.

"And we have nothing but time, at least tonight," she said, her voice low and husky. "Bear with me."

"I've never seen anyone so resolved," he said as his thumb skimmed along her cheek, his touch like a caress.

"Haven't you?" she replied as she met his ebony eyes with all the resolve she was feeling. Time's short but…" Her gaze went around the room. "We have no time to waste."

Chapter Twelve

Despite her earlier words, minutes passed.

Kate had taken a seat at the small desk while Emir had taken a position leaning against the wall. Her long legs were stretched out sideways, her body twisted as she bent over the book. The smell of pipe smoke wove into the room from the room below. The low murmur of voices and the high-pitched laugh of a child broke the quiet.

Another minute went by and then two before Kate turned and smiled at him and something caught in his chest. The sight of her dogged persistence made him think that anything was possible, that between the two of them they would find Tara.

Now she looked up with a troubled expression. "I think I've found it." She stood, the atlas in her hands.

He came over to her. His hands covered hers as he reached to take the atlas from her. The heat from her hands reminded him of how she'd felt in his arms, how he wanted her there again.

"No," she said, pulling the book back. "Let me show you."

His gaze followed her finger as she pointed to the oasis she was talking about.

She looked at him with the excitement of discovery in her eyes and something else he couldn't name. And the scent of her, coconut and something unidentifiable but equally enticing, would be his undoing as it seemed to call to him. He needed to focus.

"Emir?"

Her voice brought him back, for it was soft and husky, and oddly commanding.

"I think my hunch was right. Ajeddig is the name of an oasis in 1901. I don't remember seeing any such place on the current map, but here it's clear."

"An extinct oasis?" His gaze clashed with hers. It wasn't unheard of—water disappeared and, with it, the plants, animals and the people.

"What if there was still water left, not enough for a community but for a few people?" The question she posed hung for a moment between them. Outside the room, they could hear the low voices of their hosts.

"Wouldn't others know of it?"

"Not necessarily, not if it was obscure, hidden." She ran a finger over the area she'd been studying as if mapping their route. "Or maybe so small as to be of little interest."

He thought of the possibility she'd raised, but there were still so many unknowns. "We could drive miles out of our way in order to find out there's nothing. We could…"

"It used to be a good-size community from the looks of it. A village, anyway—a hundred people, roughly, on a guess." She spoke quickly, clearly excited by the discovery. "What better place to hide than an oasis that everyone believes no longer exists?"

She looked up at him and he leaned down and met her halfway. His lips roved over hers as he drew her into his arms. Her softness pressed against him, making him want so much more. Her mouth opened, inviting more. She was sweet and hot and… He pulled back. The last thing they needed was to be discovered, an unmarried couple making out in their host's library.

"I'm sorry," he said as he moved away from her.

"You'd better not be," she whispered huskily.

"Come here," she said, the atlas in her hands, and when he was again beside her she showed him something else that excited them both. "Two hundred miles east of here, but in the same direction as our extinct oasis. It can't be a coincidence."

"El Dewar," he said with a frown, trying not to notice the smell of her or the feel of her shoulder rubbing against his arm. It was as though fear and anger had merged with passion and become an unstoppable comet. He wanted to find his sister, kill her kidnappers and make love to Kate, and not necessarily in that order. He took her hand with his as he met her eyes. "Straight through the Sahara. There are no roads."

"Emir," she said in a soft tone, lower than normal, and one that hinted at other things. But what she had to say was all business. "Looking at this map, where the oasis is situated, if you wanted to go there, you'd have to drive through El Dewar or, at the least, near it. It's a tough drive, but we knew this wasn't going to be easy. I think we stop at El Dewar tomorrow, ask a few questions." Her eyes sparkled with excitement. "Maybe someone knows something."

Emir's pulse leaped at the possibilities.

But as he looked more closely at the landscape revealed on the old atlas, his heart sank. If this was where they had Tara, they were well defended. "If this is right—they'd be backing an almost-impermeable approach." His thumb traced the way the map outlined rises of rock and cliff that wound in a horseshoe around what had once been a desert paradise. "It would be almost impossible to get to them, sneak in, without climbing the hills behind them."

"Difficult," Kate corrected, "not impossible. I'm betting we could work our way in through the rock, over the hills—whatever. There's got to be a way. If, of course, this theory is even right."

Emir put his hands on her shoulders and kissed her. As his tongue met hers and her breasts pressed against him, it seemed like time stood still. But it was only seconds before he released her and before they took the atlas to show their host to ask him about the existence of the oasis.

"It has been uninhabited since before the days of my grandfather. Many of them moved here when it dried up. They hoped to get away from the desert," Yuften said solemnly. "I did not remember the name but the location is unforgettable."

Hours later they tried to get some sleep.

For Emir, it was impossible, for he was more aware of Kate with every second he spent in her presence. He'd kissed her one too many times when he shouldn't have kissed her at all. Maybe if he hadn't, he wouldn't want her like he'd never wanted another woman. Her mat was feet from his and a curtain divider away, and it didn't matter.

The sound of her soft breathing through the remaining hours of the night had driven him crazy. Each toss and turn, every sound, alerted him to her nearness. The cool desert air had chilled him. He'd wondered if she was cold. But there was nothing he could offer her, nothing except his own body heat, and that was unacceptable, but only because of their host. She was too near and yet too far. Worry for Tara, desire for Kate—the torrent of emotion caused the earlier headache to return, but again even the usual two aspirins were unable to stop the pounding as sunlight began to threaten the night.

They were up and preparing to leave as the sun streaked pink across the eastern sky.

TARA SHIFTED. She had to use the facilities in the worst way. She never thought an everyday necessity that one usually didn't pay much attention to would become her Achilles' heel. She squirmed, shifting onto her side, taking the pressure off her full bladder. She couldn't risk drawing attention to herself. She'd seen how her captors had looked at her as the sun rose. She'd been in this hell for over twenty-four hours.

"Find me Emir, please," she whispered to the brother who, of all of them, had been her ultimate protector, even against the gentle teasing of her other brothers. He had always stood up for her. All her brothers were her heroes, but Emir stood out among even them. Maybe because he was the eldest. It didn't matter why. What mattered was that she needed him. She'd been wrong and she'd do anything to undo what she'd done, but that was impossible, she knew that. She prayed her repentance would be enough.

She pulled her knees up tight and took a deep breath, but it didn't help. Her tormentor was heading her way. His advances had become more and more intimate and she knew that the last time she'd been lucky.

She knew him and yet he was like a stranger, a

frightening stranger. The man she remembered had been an average-size man with a glint to his dark eyes that indicated he loved a joke. And she'd told him many, at least when she'd been younger, before tragedy had struck.

Now he was lean to the point of skinny and the planes of his face were rough, wrinkled and almost feral. And then there was the scar. It wasn't the horrid scar that disturbed her the most, but more the way those dark eyes skimmed over her in an almost hungry way that made her draw back and pull her knees even closer to her chest as if that would somehow protect her.

"What do you want?" she asked and realized that she might know exactly what he wanted. She could see the lust in his eyes. There was a time when she couldn't imagine him looking at her like that and, in fact, in all her life he never had. But he didn't always see her as Tara anymore. There were times when he had, briefly, in the beginning. She'd pointed out who she was once, but she now had a bruise on her cheekbone that ached when she touched it, to remind her to not do that again.

"I've wanted you for so long and yet you only looked at him." He frowned as his knuckle skimmed her cheek.

Who? she thought. She tried to think clearly through the confusion of his words.

"Who?" she whispered. She was both scared to

engage and scared to not know what he was speaking of.

He cursed and raised his clenched fist.

She couldn't back down. She fought not to do just that.

"Your husband, of course. Who else?" He relaxed his fist and ran his hand through his grizzled, uncombed hair. He looked away from her and then turned back, a hard look in his eyes. "How did this happen?" he asked. His eyes were now, seconds later, reflecting genuine concern as he looked at the bruise on her cheekbone. It was as if he could not remember his actions from one moment to the next.

Tara fought with her control but it was so difficult to not pull away. She couldn't, not yet.

"I would have given you everything," he said, his voice soft and yet oddly hoarse. There was an edge to it that hadn't been there before. "But, no, you wanted Ruhul."

Was it possible? Ruhul Al-Nassar? Her father? Who did he think she was? Her heart was pounding so hard that she could barely think. But she knew in her gut it was critical that she was amiable and went along with whatever insane belief he had.

"Why do you shrink from me?"

She looked up at him with every ounce of willpower she had and smiled, hoping it was sweet and innocent, as her insides clenched so tight they hurt.

"I've wanted you for so long, Raja," he said gently, as if repetition would somehow get him what he wanted.

It didn't matter who she was. In the last few hours a new horror had been foisted on her. It was clear he was confused, at best. At worst, insane. She only wanted to curl up at the horror of it all. But she knew that wouldn't save her. She had to act out his obvious delusion. If he believed her to be her mother, then that was who she would be. Tara knew it was a survival tactic on her part. She'd learned that and more in a number of psychology classes.

It was a horrible role to play, a terrible thing to contemplate. She wasn't her mother.

Tara tried not to show her disgust or fear as his hand continued to stroke her cheek. She had to stop this before it was unstoppable, for he was quick this time and his hand had dropped from her cheek and was inside her blouse, under her bra. It was clear what he wanted and that this time he might not be ready to wait.

Fear combined with her full bladder and suddenly she couldn't control either. She peed her pants.

She saw his eyes look downward to the stream of urine pooling around her and saw the look of disgust on his face. He stood, took two steps back and strode back to the others.

For the first time since her horror began, Tara had the upper hand.

Hopefully her brothers would find her before her time ran out.

Chapter Thirteen

Tuesday, September 15, 10:00 a.m.

They were heading south and east with a slight wind
that was causing the unseasonal light rain to lash
against the windshield, turning the sand hitting the
glass into a paste that slid along the window, obscur-
ing the view. The Jeep's wipers beat a losing rhythm
that wasn't enough to keep the window clear. They'd
had to stop frequently to clear the clogged wipers.

The charts Kate had checked on her flight to Morocco had indicated the local weather had been unpredictable for the last few weeks. Now, that same
unpredictability, the unseasonal and unusual rain,
was making for slow going, and the abnormally cool
daytime temperature wasn't helping.

"You're okay?" he asked. His hand ran along her
wrist and the heat that ran through her at his touch
made her shiver.

"Fine." She nodded, pulling her hand free and
pushing a strand of hair back. It didn't help. Her

nerves were on edge—and not because of the assignment but because of his nearness, because of what he made her feel. It wasn't how it was supposed to be and yet that awareness had been between them from the beginning.

The Jeep rocked as Emir made a slight turn to the right, adjusting for the ridges in the sand and the breeze that was now a buffeting wind. The vehicle slid as the tires kicked up sand chewed out of the ruts it was creating.

Her finger was on the map, marking where they were and where they were going. The journey had been slow. They'd had to adjust their direction a number of times. She reached for the grab bar with her right hand as the Jeep's back tires spun and for a moment it seemed like they might get stuck in the middle of nowhere.

She looked at the compass. They were going by latitude and longitude. It was a get-back-to-basics way to travel. Even the Jeep was basic, built for this type of expedition without tracking or mapping. It reminded her how easy Google Maps had made everything.

She glanced at Emir and saw the brutal way he clasped the vehicle's steering wheel, as if it were someone's neck.

They drove in silence and yet with the promise of hope between them.

The landscape began to change as another hour

ticked by. Now the flat sand and occasional rolling dunes had become steeper and were framed by larger ridges that signaled imminent foothills. The rain was gone and the desert looked like it always had—clearly, like there'd been no rain in months.

"We're getting close," Kate said. "Maybe twenty miles from El Dewar." So far they'd made poor time, a combination of both the terrain and the weather. "No one knows the desert like the Berbers," she added as Emir navigated a small dune. "Hopefully they know something more at El Dewar that can add to what we learned at Kaher."

"I'm betting that it won't be so much a matter of them knowing but of them telling us," he said.

The side windows were closed but still the sand seemed to seep in. She pulled a tissue from the packet on the dash and wiped the corners of her eyes.

His hands tightened on the wheel as the front tires began to dig into the sand. He turned to the right and she knew he was hoping to veer out of the rut before they got stuck.

The consistency of the sand was subject to change and dependent on so many things. In an odd way, like snow. It would take all his focus to drive and navigate the unstable conditions. The desert was a challenge to drive at any time and now, with worry, little sleep and what might be a brewing storm, it was even more so.

She was relieved as the vehicle again gained traction, but ahead of them was a new difficulty. A tall bank of sand dunes stretched out on either side, with no end in sight, and blocked much of the horizon.

"In my youth we used to drive the dunes for fun," he said, looking at her with concern. "We were lucky." Minutes later his mouth tightened as he looked ahead.

"What's wrong?" Kate asked and frowned at the dunes. "Can we go around?"

"Possibly," he said. "But that could set us back hours."

"Not an option."

"I agree, but these dunes aren't going to be a cakewalk," he said. "They're whaleback dunes."

They both knew what that meant. Whaleback dunes were dunes whose front incline was hard from being buffeted by the wind. It was the back half that could pose a problem. Depending on the direction of the wind, the sand could be crumbly and difficult to navigate.

He glanced at her. "You ready to do this?"

"I've been in since the beginning," she said simply.

And with a slight smile that was more a tightening of his full lips, he slowed the Jeep. "When we reach them, watch the horizon, if it seems quite sharp at the top, then we have problems on the other side," he said.

And she knew he meant there was the possibility

of soft sand, softer than they had traveled through, and the type that could easily cause a rollover. The hope was that the sand on the other side of the dune was hard. Based on the way the wind had been buffeting them, she was sure they had a good chance of getting the latter.

He squeezed her hand and she looked down, aware of how large his hands were and, despite the gentle touch, how strong.

She pulled her hand from beneath his when all she wanted to do was to fold into his arms. There was no time for such thoughts. She forced her mind to the moment, to the challenge ahead of them.

"Let's do this," she said as if there was some chance that he wouldn't. "I'm fine," she added at the look of concern he gave her.

"You're more than fine," he said, turning his attention to the bank of dunes.

They eased over the dunes with little trouble, reaching the other side and finding the sand hard, buffeted by desert winds.

"Easier than we thought," he said.

She nodded and let go of the grab bar. It was easy driving now compared to where they had just come from. She still couldn't believe that finding Tara might be as easy as an ancient atlas and the words spoken by a dying man.

"I can see it," she said. "El Dewar."

He gripped the wheel as they recognized the first

sign of something other than the endless sea of sand. A bit of green. An oasis. The place his parents had visited with Tara and Faisal on the last trip any of them had taken as a family before tragedy had intervened and changed the course of all their lives.

His lips tightened and she bet he was thinking of all that had transpired and of the urgency that felt almost crushing.

"The summer vacation we think she was referencing in that video," Kate said.

He gave a brief nod as the Jeep bounced through a sand-packed gulley that seemed to run diagonally for a few minutes before they climbed to the top and the terrain became level again.

They drove in silence now, as they could see the oasis. It was small, as was the village it supported, and because of its isolation, she imagined that it likely saw few strangers. The usual sandstone-colored, square buildings huddled close together as if trying to escape the inhospitable desert.

Within minutes they were there.

As they got out of the Jeep, Kate was almost blinded by the sun as it reached its peak in the midday sky. But, still, it was cooler than usual for the time of year. She folded her arms across her chest as a cool breeze buffeted her, the palm trees rustling ahead of them. The fronds, moving back and forth in the center of the village, seemed, in an odd way, to almost welcome them.

A man in a fawn-colored *aselham*, the long robe skimming the tops of his feet as his sandals whispered quietly on the path that was hard-packed sand, walked past, continuing to stare as he moved. Farther away a man was filling a metal trough with water as two camels waited, reins dangling on the ground. A woman with a basket full of vegetables and a toddler clinging to her robe made her way into the center of the village, glancing back at them once and then continuing on her way. A group of women watched them and an old man smoking a cigarette was avidly following their progress. Everyone they'd seen was dressed in the traditional Berber *aselham*.

"Emir Al-Nassar," Emir said, holding out his hand as a man in fawn-colored robes approached.

"Aqil," the man returned with a slight nod of his head.

Emir didn't introduce Kate and, unlike the last village, she didn't volunteer. They needed information and shaking up the local culture in regard to their views on women wasn't going to do it.

Still, she knew Emir could feel her eyes on him. She was letting him take the lead and honoring the customs of the community.

"I heard about your sister only this morning," Aqil said in careful English. "Our internet is spotty. But, as you know, your family is well known." He shrugged as the wind tugged at his clothes. He ran a hand through his gray-speckled beard. "We were lucky to have heard when we did. The wind is pick-ing up. I doubt if we'll get a connection again today or even in the next few days. That's how it works."

"I know you usually have your ear to the ground out here," Emir said.

Aqil's attention went to Kate and he frowned.

"We can talk alone," Emir said as he followed Aqil's gaze. "Stay here," he said almost gruffly to Kate.

The command rankled her but it was Berber land and their rules. But there was one other thing she knew. It wasn't just the men who were privy to things in this isolated village; the women had a key role in society in a different way than they were used to in the West or even in the city. Knowing that, hopefully between them they would learn something.

Emir looked at her like he wanted to smile at her but didn't. Instead he let the amused smile on her face and her silence sit unacknowledged between them. But Aqil's attention had turned to a man who had just approached and Emir took the opportunity to address her.

"You'll be all right?" he asked in an undertone.

"I'll be all right," she said, although for the first time she felt slightly overwhelmed. No matter how much she'd studied, no matter her experience in Mo-rocco, on this small tract of land they were thrown back in time and place and to the reality that she was a blond-haired American woman in Western clothing. She didn't fit in.

"Speak to the elders first," he advised and motioned to an elderly woman squatting beside an open fire. "If they accept you, the others may, too." He put a hand on her shoulder. "Kate?"

She nodded. "I'm fine." But despite her words she still felt unsure and out of her element.

She took a step away as the man who had first greeted Emir came up to him.

"Come," Aqil said as he began to lead Emir. His pace fast despite his short stature. He glanced behind as he talked, as if to ensure that Emir was indeed following him.

EMIR FOLLOWED WITH one last glance and a nod to Kate as his host led him along a beaten sand path that served as a road.

A group of small boys tossed a ball back and forth and a group of women were carrying on what seemed to be a lighthearted conversation as two of them laughed. But as the men approached, they quieted and stared.

Aqil stopped in front of a one-story, square, sandstone-colored building no different than any of the others. Inside, as in the previous home they had visited, furnishings were sparse. What was different this time was that what was there was of high quality. There was an ebony, pearl-inlaid hutch and

gold-stamped figurines on various shelves throughout the room, indicating this village was doing well.

Emir removed his shoes and walked barefoot over
a rug so thick he seemed to sink as he walked across
it. This one was ruby red and in the middle sat an
intricately carved ironwood table. A trio of men sat
around the table, each with a long, thin, metal smoking stick. The smell of tobacco wove through the air
and was strangely pleasant, unlike the acrid scent
of cigarettes at home. Here it was a different smell,
warmer, in a pleasant, rather earthy kind of way that
blended with the smell of cinnamon and jasmine sift-
ing through the air from a number of incense pots
set in various corners.

He turned his attention to the man in the traditional long robe in front of them who had just joined
Aqil. Unlike his first host, this man clearly wasn't
interested in introductions.

"I wish we had met under better circumstances,"
the man said, his dark brows furrowed.

"The men you seek." He looked at Emir with a
scowl that deepened, as if challenging him to con-
tradict him. "Their group was seen not forty-eight
hours ago heading west." He took a drag from his
pipe, blew out a thin stream of smoke and continued. "They didn't stop for water nor did they enter
our village."

Emir knew that piece of information was critical.
Water was vital. No one would not stop for water in

the desert when it was available, no matter if they
carried a supply or not. Two scenarios played in his
mind—they were heading to a place they knew had
water that was relatively close, and had enough water
to get there—an oasis with enough water to keep
their small group going or…someone here had met
them with a supply.

"No one here helped them, or had any contact,"
the man said, as if he'd read Emir's mind. "And
there's nothing nearby."

"Was there…?"

"There's nothing more," the man said and turned
away from Emir. He whispered a few words to Aqil,
making it clear from his actions and poise that he
was a leader within the village.

Emir straightened. He knew he'd been dismissed,
that there was nothing further to be learned in this
room.

Chapter Fourteen

Left alone, Kate felt conspicuous and even more out of place. She tried to feign disinterest while furtively watching everything and everyone around her. It was impossible. She was a stranger, a foreigner in their midst, and she was center stage.

The children watched her curiously. One small boy came up to her and poked the back of her hand before giggling and taking a step back. He looked up at her. His dark, curly hair glistened in the sun as his curious brown eyes locked to hers. He opened his hand and held out a blue rubber ball.

"Are you going to play catch?" she said in Berber, but the boy only closed his hand, giggled and ran away. She was alone again, a curiosity in their midst. She saw a woman looking at her from her place by a pot over a cooking fire. Kate hesitated only a second before going over to her for she was the woman Emir had suggested she approach first.

"May I?" she asked, motioning to the stool. While she wasn't completely fluent in the language, she had a familiarity she'd gained through her time in the Middle East as a child with her parents when her father had worked for the American Embassy in Morocco, and again through her studies and her brief time as an exchange student.

The woman looked at her oddly. Her skin was a beautiful coffee color that glowed despite her wrinkles and advanced age. A black scarf with white embroidery partially covered her hair. Then she smiled and revealed missing teeth. She motioned for Kate to sit beside her. Her knotted fingers were quick and limber as she pinched spices from numerous tins beside her and stirred them into the pot. Kate had no idea what she was making but her stomach rumbled at the heady scent of the combined spices.

She glanced around. To her left, a group of women sat quietly watching her as they had since she'd arrived. The children played ball. The man had left with his two camels. Everything else remained the same. But something had changed. What?

Kate had never felt so out of place in her life. Despite everything she had studied, her familiarity with language and all her visits to Morocco, here she was the foreigner, the oddity with no commonality. Worse, this was the one language where she was not fluent, she could understand most of it, speak roughly but that was it. She looked back, searching for Emir, but there was no sign of him.

"Come." A woman in a mauve-and-gold *aselham*,

the hood over her head so that her forehead was covered, approached and beckoned, motioning with one hand. What Kate could see of her face and dark hair revealed a woman in her early forties with a smooth, sun-bronzed face and eyes that seemed dark, unfathomable, as if they were full of secrets.

Intrigued, she followed the woman as she skirted behind the houses to a smaller building made of the same sandstone. A brown curtain served as a door.

Kate had to bend to follow the woman through the doorway. Inside was another woman. This one was younger and dressed similarly, except her *aselham* was worn with a matching veil that was gray with gold trim. A gold tassel dangled from either side of her veil. An older woman in a cream-colored *aselham* that showed the tops of a pair of black, high-heeled boots, her long gray hair uncovered, brought her a cup of tea. Kate knew the veil was not a cultural necessity among the Berbers but more than likely worn for protection from the unseasonable weather.

She took the tea. The cup and saucer was bone china like any you'd get at home and unlike the customary Berber cup that had no handles. She sank onto the rug that covered the floor, watched the others and emulated what they did. She held the cup with both hands, not the usual way to hold what seemed a traditional teacup. Despite her studies and everything she knew about Morocco and the Middle East, she'd never seen a tribe such as this that seemed to dance between traditional customs and ones that, she guessed, weren't acquired from popular culture but distinctly their own.

"They won't tell him the truth," the younger woman said in a soft voice. "He was paid too well."

The oldest of them clicked her tongue, an oddly loud sound in the ensuing silence. She held up her hand. "Enough of such talk."

"It's true," the younger woman persisted. "They will not say anything."

Kate put her cup down and met the older woman's eyes. She took a chance that these women knew why they were here and they might very well know where Tara was. "Sheikka Tahriha Al-Nassar may die if we don't find her soon."

Silence hung within the room for what seemed like minutes and might have only been seconds.

Finally the woman who had led her there said, "I will say what I know but you are to tell no one what has been said within these walls until you leave this village." Her gaze was intense, serious. "This is between us. The women here and no more."

"I promise," Kate said sincerely.

"I tell you this. I will breach the will of our men only because one of our sisters is in danger," she said. The words were spoken in careful and precise English and because of that they seemed even more ominous.

Kate held back a shiver.

The woman squatted beside Kate and pulled her veil back, revealing fresh, clear skin that was much more youthful than Kate had imagined without the veil casting shadows along the sides of her face.

As she listened, Kate could feel the tension tightening in her gut and the implications of it all made her want to cry for Emir, for his family. But, first, she knew that the man who was intent on destroying the house of Al-Nassar must be stopped.

"Do you know where they were going?" Kate asked.

"No." She hung her head but when she looked up and her lips were set as if she'd made a decision. "That is all."

Kate nodded and stood.

"Thank you," she said. She wanted to shake the woman's hand but she knew that wouldn't be acceptable.

She was surprised when the woman offered her own hand. They shook and, with a nod, the woman led her outside before she disappeared down a narrow break between dwellings.

Where the woman had gone there was now only a goat, who lifted his head from a pail from which he was placidly eating and then turned back to his food as if whatever was going on was of little interest to him. Two children chased past her, their childish laughter no different from children anywhere, as dust rose up under their bare feet and the sun beat down on her as if nothing was wrong. Just behind them a shadow drifted between the buildings and she saw a young man, bearded, dressed in a brown robe. Their eyes met as if he were analyzing her. Then, as if she wasn't supposed to see him, he too disappeared.

She turned as a shudder ran through her, a combination of dread and determination. They'd find Sheikka Tahriha if it was the last thing she did. Despite everything, and maybe because of everything she'd learned, she had the feeling she was no longer welcome. She felt like there were eyes watching her. She needed to find Emir so they could get out of here—now.

Chapter Fifteen

"Emir!" Kate's voice called from behind him.

He turned from his conversation with one of the older men to see her hurrying toward him, her face pale, her hair escaping the ponytail, as usual.

A couple of small girls shadowed her footsteps, imitating her walk and her voice as they giggled. She looked back at them and then at Emir with a pained expression. He'd never seen her look so uncomfortable, so out of place.

She took his arm, her eyes pleading. "Let's go," she whispered.

He nodded at her. They were done here.

But there was something in her voice that said there was more.

"What's going on Kate?" he asked as they approached the Jeep parked just outside the oasis. He looked around. They were alone.

"Kate?"

She turned and, just like that, he felt like he was drowning in the rich blue of her eyes. They glistened with excitement, tears—he wasn't sure what. He held himself back from doing what he ached to do—take her in his arms. They might be alone but there still could be eyes that watched them and he wanted to get moving, they both did, even though it was clear something was troubling her.

He had the Jeep in gear and the village was far behind them before he asked, "What is it?"

"You may know one of the men who took Tara," she said.

The husky tone in her voice would have been alluring at another time. Again, the thought leaped at him out of nowhere, broadsiding him, enraging him with its lack of control.

"At least, that's what the woman I spoke to implied. But more than that, he knew your parents," she went on before he could say anything. "Maybe he worked for you. I don't know."

Shock ran through Emir and left him momentarily speechless.

"That's impossible," he growled. It implied betrayal of the worst kind. His head pounded and dread settled through him as if deep in his core he realized that, despite all their precautions, just like Tara's abduction, what she said was very possible.

"Is it?"

"That's crazy. We screened all our employees. They're all loyal, trustworthy, even friends." He couldn't believe it, wouldn't. In that moment he only wanted to fight the implication with every-thing in him.

"I know you ran a check through all the past and current employees. But, Emir, it's possible. What I find interesting is that it hasn't happened sooner. People envy wealth like yours—even those who call themselves friend."

"Who are you talking about?"

"While you were with the men, a woman took me aside. She told me about a man who had vis-ited the village six years ago. He'd stopped for water and her husband had offered him a smoke and food. Her husband knew the man's family—they had once been from that tribe. She could only say that he was middle-aged, Arabic, and attractive in a tired kind of way. He said at the time, that the House of Al-Nassar was cursed. She wasn't privy to everything he said but she saw money change hands for their silence. What she remembers most is how he spoke with an almost rabid hatred of the House of Al-Nassar and kept repeating how someday he would bring it down. She remembers the name Raja."

"My mother's name!" The Jeep lurched and swerved.

She looked at him with concern in her eyes before continuing. "At the time she forgot about it, as much of what she'd heard made no sense. She'd thought it the crazy ranting of a nut. She'd left it up to the men to handle and, since her husband passed, she'd long forgotten about it until today. Your surname reminded her. In fact—"

The satellite phone rang, interrupting her and startling them both.

"Yeah?" Emir answered. He gripped the phone like he might never let it go. "What do you have, Zaf?" he asked as he stopped the Jeep.

"I've gone through all the past employees back five years," Zafir said.

"Not you, too." But Emir knew it was necessary. He'd known this situation had always been possible. But even the possibility had never stopped him from caring for the people he hired. Many of them had worked for his family for years. His employees were friends and sometimes even family. He couldn't imagine now—or more aptly didn't want to consider—that anyone he cared about would threaten him or anyone he loved.

"No matches," Zafir went on, unaware of his thoughts. "Not that we expected there would be."

Emir's knuckles were white.

Kate's hand settled on his wrist as if, again, that would somehow calm him. Oddly, it did, but the feel of her skin on his did other things, too, things that had no place there or with the shock of what she'd implied, still so fresh. He shook her hand off, concentrating on his phone call. But a glance at her face made him wish he hadn't done so, so thoughtlessly.

"I don't know, Zaf. And, as far as our current

employees? There's no one working for us with a grudge. No one in need of money—at least, not to that extent. They're loyal to a fault. I don't know where else to take this."

Emir could feel Kate's eyes still on him.

"Just a moment."

"Nothing turned up. He went back five years," he said to Kate. Unfortunately, with the satellite phone there was no ability to put it on speaker, so he had to juggle two conversations and relay between Zafir and Kate.

"Can he take it back another five? We need to talk...can you call him back?" she asked.

"You know there's no guarantee of a signal," he reminded her.

She nodded. "All right." Her lips thinned as if it pained her to say the next words. "When was your parents' accident?"

Emir frowned. It was a subject that was too painful to talk about and, after the police report had been filed, the incident had been filed in his own mind, as well. "Over six years ago." His gut clenched. He didn't like where this was going, didn't know if he wanted to hear it, but he had no choice. Tara's life depended on him.

"But when, exactly, and who was with them?"

"Why, Kate?"

"It wasn't the only time that man was there, at the village. He was there the year of the accident and he was there recently. And this time she heard his first name."

"Damn it, Kate, who was he?"

"Ed."

The barren reaches of desert stretched in front of them and it was only that that kept his outrage contained. He didn't look in the rearview mirror, either, for behind them was the place that had moved them to a truth he feared might change everything he thought he knew. He took a breath and then glanced at her.

"What's going on?" he heard Zafir ask. "K.J. was asking about the accident?"

"Hang on, Zaf," he said into the phone.

"Get Zafir to check who was on staff the year of your parents' accident and also if there was anyone with them, or who they had contact with that day." She frowned. "I know some of that will be impossible to recollect, but if there was someone with them…"

"Ed," Emir said with no hesitation. "Their bodyguard. Simohamed Khain. We called him Ed," he said. "And the driver, of course. Ed was the only survivor," he said gravely.

Kate could see that his mind was there, in that moment on that fateful day when he'd learned his parents' fate and when everything had changed for him and his siblings.

"Run a check on Ed," she said.

He nodded grimly, his jaw tense and his dark eyes narrowed. "Zaf, did you hear?" Emir asked his brother.

"I'm missing most of this and I think it's a waste of time, Em."

"Yeah, well, she's right. We can't afford to toss anything out at this point. Call as soon as you know something," Emir said before he clicked off.

He swung around to face Kate. "What are you suggesting?"

"It's not what I was suggesting," she said. "It was what I was told."

"You think the accident that killed my parents was not accidental at all—is that what you're implying?"

"I don't know," she replied.

His jaw tightened. "It's one thing to have Zaf do a search, but to think a man who was like a brother to my father…on the basis of a name similarity."

"Wait. There's more." She turned away, likely gathering her thoughts before facing him, pain obvious in her eyes.

He didn't want her sympathy and he didn't want to hear what she had to say, either, for he knew that whatever it was might be a betrayal from which his family would never recover. He prayed he was wrong.

"So you think—"

"Wait." She held up her hand. "The woman in El Dewar said that the last time he visited, a few months ago, there was something new, a burn down the entire left side of his face." She looked at him with eyes full of compassion that almost did him in. "That's not all. She was wearing a bracelet that looked very much like the one you said Tara had inherited from your mother."

It was like he'd been sucker punched.

"I'm sorry, Emir."

He didn't want her apology. He didn't want to look at the sympathy in her eyes. He wanted to take her into his arms and make her stop talking, make her stop causing him to face possibilities that threatened everything he believed.

"There were two," he murmured. "I thought the second was destroyed in the accident. In fact, until now, I'd forgotten about it." He looked away. When he turned back to face her, he was more determined than ever to make the men who had taken Tara pay. "The woman you spoke to…"

She nodded. "Had what I think is the second bracelet. When I noticed the similarity, I asked her where she got it. She said their visitor had dropped it, and by the time she found it, he was gone. I'm almost positive it's a match." She stopped, concern on her face.

Emir's right hand was clenched in a fist. "Ed's face on the left side was burned pretty badly. He said he struggled to open Mother's door—to get her out."

"My informant was pretty sure it was a burn scar.

She said she'd seen plenty in the village from the cooking pots and such."

"The woman heard him talking to himself as he was preparing to leave. She said that she would always remember the words, for they were spoken with hatred. She said he was muttering that he would make the sheikka pay."

"Make her pay? What had Tara done to him?"

"Was it Tara he was referring to?"

Shock rolled through him at what she might be implying. It made no sense. "Who else would he mean?"

She shrugged. "You said he tried to get your mother free from the vehicle. Why not your father? Why didn't he mention him? Attempt to save him?"

"What are you saying?"

"I'm not sure. I…"

"Kate…" He could hear his heart beat in anticipation of what she might say next. He wanted to put his hand over her mouth and not allow her to say the words he sensed would change everything he thought he knew.

"Did Ed act strangely around your mother? I mean, before the accident?"

"I…no, he was close to my father. My mother and he were formal with each other any time I saw them. An employee and a friend, he never crossed that line…"

"Never?"

"No." He shook his head. "But I remember Mother saying she didn't like him. She asked Father to fire him. That was just before the accident. Damn. She said he was taking liberties and by that I thought she meant treating Father as a friend..."

"When instead could it have been that Ed was making advances on her? Could he have been in love, lust, whatever, with your mother—and she knew or possibly only suspected?"

Kate's blue eyes were troubled and yet full of passion. He couldn't help but touch her cheek and press his lips to hers, in a desperate attempt to alleviate some of his pain. She sank into his kiss, her tongue meeting his, her breast soft, her nipple hard against his palm. He wanted her as much as he wanted all the pain of this new discovery to go away.

He let her go.

She gave him a slow seductive smile and then swung right back into business. "I don't think we can afford to discount this. If we know who Tara's kidnappers are, what motivates them, going in..."

"We have a better chance against them," he finished. "If this is true, what has he been doing all these years? He hasn't been in our employ since the accident." Emir frowned. "We paid him out a compensation package." His fist clenched. "How could he have hidden it...?" But he knew how criminals such as this might act. He just couldn't imagine that someone he had known and trusted...

"Biding his time," Kate replied. "And, I suspect, slowly losing his mind."

Emir raked his fingers through his hair. "Then you're saying that Tara's dealing with a madman?"

"Possibly," she said quietly.

And both of them knew they'd just hit worst-case scenario.

DESPITE THE FACT that it was still daylight, Tara was so tired she could barely keep her eyes open. But she was too afraid to sleep. It was the only reason she could think that he had been able to come up to her, to surprise her without her realizing he was there.

His thick, dark hair was curly and too long, but it framed a face that might have been handsome, had he not been either so thin or so twisted. The intent in his eyes took away from any potential beauty in his face. His mouth curved in a self-satisfied smile that sent a chill down her spine and had her shifting away from him.

"It's been a long time," he said softly.

Tara blinked, as if that would clear her vision, as if that might change the reality of the man before her. "Why? Why have you done this?"

"Why? You dare to ask that as if you didn't know—you, with your life of privilege. I will be glad to end it when it comes to that."

"But what about the money?"

"What about the money, my foolish little princess, looking down at all of us, thumbing your nose at…"

"You taught me the rules of American football. You—" She broke off, unable to say any more. When he was so near, she tensed to the point she forgot to breath. She took a breath. He seemed to realize in this moment that she was not her mother. It was as though his reality shifted from one moment to the next.

"You were easier to deceive than your brothers, but you all came around."

She stared into a face that was barely familiar, into eyes that were filled with hate, and at a man that it was now clear she had never known. She willed herself to not shrink back, to not show weakness, for in her gut she knew he wanted that as much as he wanted the money.

He reached for her as she twisted away, but it was impossible to escape. The rope that held her only allowed her to move so far.

His knuckle ran down the side of her face. "You never wanted me, did you, despite everything? It was always him." He looked at her as he dropped back on his heels and stood. "I can keep you forever. He will never find you and I will bleed him dry." He ran a thumb along the ridge of her collarbone. His touch was chilling despite the fact that two layers of cotton fabric lay between him and her.

"My brothers…"

He looked at her with angry, confused eyes.

"You call your sons, brothers?"

Tara's sleep-deprived brain didn't have an immediate comeback. She fought not to shrink back as the horror returned and her brain made sense of what he had said. Again, he thought that she was her mother. He'd slipped back into his mad delusion where she became her mother. A chill ran down her spine and she forced herself to look at him.

"He'll never agree," she said, not giving names, meaning her brothers and especially Emir, and leaving it open to his interpretation.

"Then you, my dear, must die. Not now," he said as she looked at him with all the panic she was feeling. "I, of course, will shed tears. But there's really no other way."

She shivered as the chill of the day and the thought of the inevitable night combined with thoughts of her potential destiny, and all of it settled harsh and heavy in her heart.

Chapter Sixteen

Tuesday, September 15, 3:00 p.m.

The village of El Dewar was long gone. The clouds had moved in and the sky was ominous-looking, and the wind was again picking up.

Twenty minutes later they'd stopped for a quick break and were just about to head back to the Jeep when a billowing cloud of sand to the northwest caught Emir's attention. The buzz of an approaching engine followed and he met Kate's quizzical look.

"More than likely, a dirt bike, from the sounds of it," he said.

But it was the unmistakable sound of a gunshot and a thud of a bullet hitting metal that had them diving to the sand.

"Whoever it is, they're targeting the Jeep," Kate said in an undertone as if silence mattered.

There was nothing to say. Emir knew stopping had been a mistake. The dunes had provided camouflage and there'd been no one else around, or so he'd thought. But in trying to provide privacy for Kate he'd inadvertently made them vulnerable. There was nothing to do now but deal with the consequences.

They needed to somehow get back to the Jeep. Right now, it was too far away to be of any help. They'd have to use the small dune beside them for cover. Emir motioned with one arm but Kate was already moving that way, her gun in her hand, keeping as far down as possible as she moved. They didn't return fire, for they didn't want to alert their attacker to where they were. So far whoever it was had only fired at the Jeep. There was still a chance that whoever was shooting hadn't spotted them yet, hadn't realized they'd left their vehicle.

Emir moved forward, head down, trying to keep himself between the shooter and Kate, but she refused to be anything but an equal participant. Exactly as he'd expect from any of his agents, but as much as he hated to admit it, even to himself, Kate was different.

Another shot, this time to their left and over their heads. It was clear now that the shooter knew they weren't at the Jeep. Suddenly there was silence. Emir frowned. With both hands on the Glock, he shifted to his left, motioning Kate to follow.

They were now maybe twenty feet from the Jeep.

A bullet hit the dune just behind them and kicked up a small cloud of sand. Kate motioned with her hand that she was going to move right and along the dune.

Emir nodded as he covered her progress. But suddenly they weren't alone. The roar of the bike engine bore down on them as it flew over one dune, coming closer, only sixty feet away. He fired at it, kicking up sand and causing the biker to swerve right and away from them. Emir fired again and this time the driver lost control. The bike toppled, skidding on its side as the driver landed on his feet, his rifle in the sand behind him. They needed to get to the Jeep and they had a minute or less to do it before he was back on his bike.

Kate fired once, twice, but the angle was wrong—a dune protected him.

"Run!" Emir commanded unnecessarily as they both ran, keeping low and moving fast. They launched themselves into the Jeep.

"Go!" Kate yelled. It was another unnecessary command for he had the accelerator to the floor. The Jeep sped forward, pelting sand behind them as they flew over a dune, swerving back and forth to avoid any shots from the biker.

Kate turned and fired multiple times.

"We want him alive, if possible," Emir shouted over the roar of the engine and knew that the odds were slight that that was going to happen, especially if they both wanted to come out of this alive.

She nodded and, oddly, despite the intensity of

the situation, despite the fact that their attention was fixed on their attacker, she turned and smiled at him.

Damn, he thought. She was enjoying this.

The biker was catching up. The bike swerved around them, dodging Kate's shots, and a bullet cracked the back side window. Plumes of sand kicked up from the bike and masked their attacker's identity.

Another dirt bike roared over a dune just behind them. Now there was one bike in front and one behind. They had a fifty-foot gap between them and their assailants on either side.

Kate dropped the empty magazine, reloaded her Colt M-1911 and took aim at the second biker. She fired and a quick glance in the rearview mirror said she hadn't been lucky. The bike was still hot on their tail. The driver's face was hidden behind a red cloth that covered his face and protected him from the sand that billowed up around him.

"He's not wearing a helmet," Kate muttered. She took aim and fired once, then twice. "We'll be able to take him out that much easier."

Emir had one hand on the wheel, while with the other he held his Glock. It was almost impossible to steer and aim, but he took a shot at the first biker— at least he could keep him off balance, having to react, giving Kate a chance to line up a better shot.

The second biker was swerving now, seeming to lose control. They were still bracketed between two attackers.

"Hang on!" Emir shouted as he veered right and the Jeep sailed across the desert sand, the wind seeming to howl around them. But neither bike was stopping. Instead both bikes changed direction, one heading in a diagonal path straight at them and the other tailing them but quickly coming up on the other side.

The first biker was again ahead of them. But as he lifted his rifle to fire—the bike skidded sideways and the rider was thrown. He was up on his feet as Kate took aim and fired again. Emir fired a second shot. Sand kicked up around the biker and then he was at the bike. He lifted the rifle, aiming at them as Kate fired, and the rifle snapped out of his hands, slewing along the sand.

"He's unarmed!" she shouted.

Emir swung in the direction of the unarmed biker, the Jeep's engine roaring, sand kicking up behind them. It was a race as to who would get to the gun first, but just as suddenly as Emir swerved, the man pulled a revolver from his belt. Kate was hanging out of the window now and all Emir wanted to do was to pull her in to safety. Instead he had to trust her.

A shot screamed off the side of the Jeep and another echoed off the hood.

"Got him!" she shouted.

The words had barely left her mouth before the remaining dirt biker came ripping over the dune, full throttle, as if he'd been waiting for this moment.

Emir swerved the Jeep, gunning the engine as much as he dared, angling, making them less of a target while Kate kept their remaining attacker busy having to swerve right and then left as he dodged her shots.

No matter her difficulty in the Berber village, here, Kate was good. It was a rogue thought and one he couldn't entertain as he veered again, shadowing the maneuvers of the biker, making them a more difficult target.

He could see Kate, both hands on her handgun, her eyes narrowed. She pulled the trigger. The bike skidded, throwing the rider as the bike rolled down a small sand dune.

"He's not moving," Emir said, looking in the rearview mirror at the fallen biker.

He looked at Kate. Her face was flushed and there was a troubled look to her eyes as she glanced at him, and he realized the earlier smile had been all about the joy of the chase. The kill was another matter. He gripped the wheel as he turned in the direction of the first downed biker.

As they approached, and the Jeep slowed, Kate was out, crouching, her handgun raised and ready to fire. The biker lay sprawled thirty feet ahead.

Emir threw the Jeep into Park and followed Kate, his gun in both hands. But the biker still wasn't moving.

Kate looked back, nodded when she saw Emir in

position just behind her and shifted to her left, carefully moving forward until she reached the body. She pushed the biker's shoulder with her foot—nothing. She squatted and turned the body over. It was a man, thin, with a scruff of dark beard, maybe thirty years old. "He was at El Dewar. I remember him standing between the houses. It was just a moment and then he vanished."

Emir could see the man's rifle was thrown five feet away and that his body lay in an awkward position. It was clear without bending to check that his neck had been broken.

"There're no more answers here," Kate said grimly. She strode over to the bike that lay eight feet away from the corpse. A worn leather bag hung over the seat. She opened it, her expression grim, and pulled out a water bottle and a cell phone. "A disposable phone," she said, turning it on. "Nothing."

Emir came up beside her. "What are you saying? That he's not one of the kidnappers?"

"I don't think so, but he's obviously not innocent. He knows something and it seems like he was trying to prevent us from going any farther."

"We're not finished here yet," Emir said grimly. "Let's go back. Maybe there're answers there." He shrugged in the direction of the other downed biker.

Five minutes later they were at the body of the second biker. Like the first, he was dead. But, unlike the first, they didn't recognize him at all and he carried nothing but his pistol, a water jug and an extra magazine for his weapon.

Kate stood and took a step back.

The wind was quickly picking up and already it was whipping at their clothes and driving sand into their faces. Emir slipped his sunglasses on and she did the same.

"We're going to have to leave him here," he said with a final look at the body. "I'll alert Zaf when the satellite connects again." The satellite had been down since they'd begun this leg of their journey.

His heart was pounding. No matter how many times he was in a gun battle, he never liked them because the outcome always meant someone was going to die. Yet, when he looked over at Kate, he saw the flush on her cheeks and a slight curve to her lips, as if she was about to smile.

As the wind whipped a strand of hair across her face and she turned to look at him with eyes that sang with excitement, he realized that, no matter how much he disliked killing, there was one thing he'd never admitted. That it was eclipsed by the heady power of the afterglow, of being the one still alive. They might have killed two men but the alternative was that they would have been killed themselves. The silent communication between them had reminded him of that and he knew in that moment he couldn't have asked for a better partner.

They drove in silence for a while. Their only goal

was to get as close to the oasis undetected as they could before night came or the storm hit—whichever came first.

The ringing of the satellite phone made Kate jump. "We're back in business," she said with relief in her voice.

Emir picked up the phone before the second ring ended. "What do you have?"

"Ed hasn't been working security like he led us to believe. In fact, I'm not sure what he's been doing. I'm doing more digging. Two things. First, I think Tara's kidnappers are on to us," Zafir said. "They haven't followed up with any additional demands. I'm getting worried and I think it was a mistake to go after them."

"We didn't have a choice," Emir said and frustration wove through the words.

"Okay, look, keep your eyes open. You've got bigger trouble coming. There's a sandstorm forecasted. You need to take shelter. Weather reports look like you might have another clear hour, maybe less."

"Less. It's starting up already." Emir's tone gritted. He told Zafir what had happened and about the bodies they'd left behind.

"Give me your coordinates," Zafir growled. "I don't like any of this"

A minute later Emir turned to Kate. "We're going to have to camp for the night." It was something they'd both known for a while now. "If we didn't

suspect we were heading into a storm, Zaf's confirmed it."

The earlier excitement was gone. Kate's full lips
were tight with tension. She gripped the dash, staring out over the desert with a grim look as if he'd
sentenced her to life instead of one night.

And he knew her worry, knew it tenfold, for it
meant his sister must spend one more night alone
with her kidnappers.

His jaw tightened as he navigated a rut. The Jeep
bounced and the tires spun as they hit hard, flat sand.
As they came out of the dip, the wind began to whip
around them. They had no choice. They didn't stand
a chance in unfamiliar terrain in a sandstorm.

Emir shifted the Jeep down a gear and veered
left, taking the dune that loomed ahead at an angle,
as it was steeper than any of the others they had yet
to encounter. Straight-on and he could visualize the
rollover that would follow. They were close to the
oasis. According to Kate's last coordinates, less than
ten miles away.

"We need shelter!" Kate yelled five minutes later
over the roar of the wind. "We can't go any farther."
Sand pelted the vehicle and it was getting more and
more difficult to see. But, according to the map, there
were sandstone cliffs on the other side of this ridge.
Before they'd been attacked, they'd been taking it
slow, scouting the area—noting the weaknesses, the
strengths, buying time. Now they were about to be

swallowed in the storm if they didn't get to shelter quickly. Just as that thought ran through his mind, the first shot rang out.

"What the—?" Kate bit off the rest of her comment as she swung around in the direction of the shot, her gun in her hand and crouching in her seat, taking what cover she could.

Emir swerved right then left, taking them dangerously close to a rollover. He looked over at Kate who was on her knees as she put herself in a position to defend them both. He couldn't have asked for a better person to ride shotgun.

"Go left," Kate shouted over the din of the Jeep's engine and the wind. "I think they're using that break to the right between the dunes." She glanced left. "This storm is going to be our cover pretty soon."

He couldn't agree with that assessment more, but all he could do now was get them as far away as possible.

She was firing blindly through the partially opened window, but there was only a distant shot returned and that indicated that the shooter might be on foot.

"So much for sneaking in," Emir said, his hands clenching the wheel as he realized what this could mean.

"We'll work around it, Emir." She looked at him with lips tight. She was perched on the seat as if poised to launch. They were over a mile from the first shot and, through the waves of sand and gusts of wind, he could see the rise of a hill to their right. The storm had intensified and was now driving sand so thick that there was no going much farther. They were as far away as the storm would allow.

They were so close to Tara and yet so far.

Chapter Seventeen

"There." Kate pointed as a bank of low-rise cliffs appeared to their right.

"It should work," he agreed as he fought to keep the Jeep moving in the right direction. The sand was beginning to act like water as it moved with the wind that churned it.

The visibility had rapidly decreased. Some storms could come out of nowhere, swallowing you in a sea of sand, while others were slower moving and, often, longer lasting. This one wasn't hitting them out of nowhere but it was rapidly getting worse.

Within minutes he had the Jeep angled in the direction the wind was coming from, using it to act as a barrier.

"We'll set up the tent beside the Jeep," he said. "We could stay in the Jeep if I thought this thing was going to blow over quickly, but all signs look like it might run through the night." A gust of wind hammered him from behind, pushing him forward. He looked at Kate, who was struggling to double her ponytail to keep it from whipping against her face. The scarf she'd been using had blown away minutes ago.

They wrestled with the tent to get the anchor lines secured.

Finally, inside the tent, Kate shivered, clutching her arms. "It's getting cold."

It was late afternoon but the temperature had plummeted and inside the tent it was only slightly less chilly than outside.

He tossed her a blanket. "Thanks," she said as she wrapped it around her shoulders. "One night, not too bad," she said. "Maybe the kidnappers will get in touch with Zafir by then. I don't know why they're waiting."

"Any number of reasons, but thinking of any of them isn't going to help us."

"Maybe," she said with doubt in her voice. "I don't think that last attack was planned. I mean, they shot at us twice and the second was so distant. I think whoever it was, unlike the bikers, they were shooting blind."

"As in we could have been anyone and not someone necessarily after them."

"Exactly."

"I suppose we'll soon find out once the storm is over." He knelt by the small, portable heater. "We'll get this going and it should warm up fast." He glanced at her with a smile. "Just like home."

"Home with dehydrated stew for supper," she said with a smile more poignant than humorous.

"Not even that," he said. "We have no stove. Unless you want it cold, but I'm not sure how that will work with cold water…"

"Stop," she said with a laugh.

The storm had intensified too fast and they had taken what they could from the Jeep. He'd managed to grab a bag with food supplies and she'd gotten blankets, but after that the storm had taken charge. The camp stove among a few other things had been left behind.

They had shelter and, more importantly, they were alive. They had lived and others had died.

She wasn't sure how it happened but suddenly she was in his arms and his lips were on hers. Her heart beat wildly as he held her tight against him and she could feel him hard and ready against her belly. His lips were warm and oddly soft in a demanding, masculine way as they parted hers, and her heart pounded in time with his.

She wanted to hold him tighter and demand more. And yet it all seemed too soon and too much. For the first time she had thoughts that hadn't occurred to her before. He was her boss. Her job mattered. Sex with the boss wasn't the best career plan she'd ever had.

"No." She shook her head. "I can't."

His knuckle ran along the edge of her cheek, caressing it, as his tongue tasted the edge of her lips. "What's wrong?" he asked thickly, his desire still hard between them.

"No, Emir. Not now." Why did she say that? Not ever was what she meant to say as the wind howled and the tent rocked and sand pelted against the canvas.

He caressed her breast.

She couldn't have wanted him any more than she did in that moment. Instead she pulled back, forcing him to let her go.

"You're my boss," she muttered.

His dark eyes raked her face but he said nothing.

She moved away from him but the tent wasn't large. She found herself next to the heater, a heat that was safer than the kind of heat he offered.

"We need to get some food, get some sleep and make a plan," she said.

An awkward silence seemed to descend after those words. She looked at him from beneath her lashes. His back was to her and he was going through their supplies. Apparently he wasn't fazed by rejection.

"Here's one of your demands met," he said, holding up a can. His expression was placid, like nothing had happened between them.

He tossed her a can of soup followed by a spoon and she peeled the metal lid back. Despite the fact that it was cold and, as a result, slightly congealed, it was exactly what she needed.

Ten minutes later she set the empty can aside. The storm was still going full force and as the wind pushed and pulled at the canvas, the noise was almost alarming. It was dark except for the occasional flicker of a flashlight they used to navigate the space. The wind rocked the tent and she wondered if it would hold.

"Ignore it," he advised. "We'll be fine."

But there was pain in his eyes and she knew that he thought of Tara.

"We'll all be fine," she said. "Tara, too."

He didn't say anything. Instead he handed her a tin of rice pudding.

"No." She laughed. "There's something about rice in pudding—no."

"Don't know what you're missing."

He took a spoonful of pudding that some employee had thrown into the kit and grimaced as he swallowed. He held out his spoon. "You sure?" he asked with a smile.

"From the look on your face, yes," she said with a laugh and then immediately turned serious. "We're seven miles from the oasis. That's what I got from what I saw of landmarks before the storm hit and from matching it on the map," she said thoughtfully.

He put the tin down. "We could walk in once the storm…"

"A mile of that is going to be a fairly challenging climb through the cliffs that are backing the oasis. Not wise in the dark." She paused. "I've been thinking about the kidnappers. They've been playing you, taking their time."

"And?"

"I think we buy time, make them nervous. Play the game they're playing right back at them. We put ourselves in position to move on them by nightfall." She looked at her watch. It was now only seven. "Tomorrow."

"And Tara has to spend another day and night with them. Anything could happen, they could kill…"

"They need her, Emir. I think we put her in less danger if we bide our time, make them sweat a bit more, than if we try to move in without any idea of the environment in which they're holding her. Tomorrow we'll be prepared and we can use the night to our advantage."

Hours later she slept and awoke to see that it wasn't quite as dark, that the storm had abated and that she was cold. She looked over. Emir was sitting up, his gaze thoughtful.

She sat up, too. "What's going on?"

"Not much," he replied. "Almost daylight. We've got about an hour."

"Did you get any sleep?" she asked as she blinked and rubbed her eyes.

"No." He shook his head. "You got some sleep anyway."

"I did," she replied as she ran a hand through her hair. "I must look a mess."

"No," he said softly, his eyes intense as they swept over her. "You look beautiful."

"Beautiful?" she repeated. She'd just been through a gunfight, a sandstorm—killed a man. No, two.

"They needed to die, Kate," he said as if he'd read her mind, as if he knew that despite the thrill of battle she was not a killer. "It made me sick the first time and the second. It makes me sick every time," he said.

"I threw up the first time," she admitted. "And almost quit."

"I'm glad you didn't," he said softly, meeting her eyes. His were like molten chocolate, the look in them more of that of a lover than of a friend or colleague or even boss.

"I've never met anyone like you, Kate," he said in a gravelly whisper.

She shivered.

"You're cold. The heater isn't much. Come here," he said and he could hear the edge in his voice.

He moved closer to her until he was right beside her. He lifted the blanket from his shoulders and brought it around both of them, and pulled her close to him, using his body to warm her. "Neither of us will be any use to Tara if we use all our energy trying to keep warm."

But it was only a few minutes of them sitting like that, with her pressed against his side so tight that he could feel the softer contour of her breast, that he knew it had been a mistake. Nature hadn't built enough restraint in him to hold a woman more sensual than any he'd met before and just keep her warm, or for that matter a woman he'd been attracted to since he'd first set eyes on her.

He tipped her face up and kissed her long and hard, his tongue tasting her, relishing it all; the sweet taste of the cinnamon gum she'd chewed just after awakening, the hot feel of her tongue as it mated with his, the sleek feel of her skin, all awakening a desire in him that ached to be appeased.

He took a deep breath and reminded himself of why he was there, that she was his employee, as she had reminded him—a partner for now. She couldn't be anything else. And none of that mattered. For the beat of his heart told another story.

"I want you," he whispered as if all the kisses that had come before hadn't already told her that.

"You're my boss, and my career…"

She looked at him with a desire that had him using all his willpower to hold back.

The rise of her breast seemed no more than a lover's kiss, a soft caress against his upper arm. He reached out tentatively, his palm brushing the seductive softness.

"I want to be so much more," he whispered. "The rest doesn't matter."

Her breath was a small purr of pleasure as her hand slipped under his shirt, skimmed the side of his ribs and moved down as if his words had given her permission.

His hands dropped lower, pulling her tight against him, flipping onto his back with her on top as he kissed her with every ounce of enthusiasm and feeling she gave him. His hand grazed the edge of her breast as it seductively pressed against him and his want pressed against her thigh.

She shuddered.

"You're still cold." He raised himself on an elbow, reaching for the blanket that had dropped to the side.

She took his wrist, even as she shook her head. "Don't stop."

He rolled over so that he was on top of her, blocking the cold tendrils of the breeze that seemed to find its way inside the tent. Her curves were pressed more tightly against him. His hand slid under her T-shirt, undoing the front hook of her bra, freeing her breast into his hand. One hand cupped a breast while the other pulled the T-shirt over her head, the bra followed.

She moaned as her nipple tightened beneath his fingers.

He took one nipple in his mouth, his tongue tormenting her in tiny caresses as he toyed with one and then the other. She twisted, rising up as if to meet his hardness, as if that would get them what they both wanted sooner.

"I can't wait," he said thickly as he unzipped her pants; his hand slipped under her panties to find her wet. She quivered as his fingers parted her.

Soon she was bare beneath him and her hand was reaching for his zipper.

His hand slipped between them, covering hers, stilling it.

He stood, took off his pants and was again pulling the blanket up around them, as their body heat was trapped by the blanket and combined with the heat of desire finally succeeded in warding off the desert chill.

"Now," she said as she rose to meet him and clung to him as he entered her as quickly as he'd seduced her. Yet, in the hot and cold of the desert, where life was both tenacious and fragile, somehow it felt right.

But it was only when she rolled over and took command did he wish that time was not a short commodity, because for blissful minutes the nightmare that had been over fifty hours in the making was soothed twice in the most blissful way possible.

"I'm sorry," she said when she laid by his side sometime later.

It was a strange comment and one he supposed he

should have been making, but he wasn't sorry. He'd been attracted to her from the beginning—wrong place and wrong time, it didn't matter—he wanted this to happen.

"I'm not," he said and there was a hoarse edge to his voice. He sat up and snapped the top off one of their water bottles, took a long, thirsty swig and then offered it to her. "It was bound to happen."

"What do you mean by that?" she demanded as she stood, naked and unconcerned, her hair loose, caressing the edges of her breasts, her face flushed from his kisses. "I was just sorry we didn't have more time."

"Really?" Desire raced hot and wild through him. "You're damn sexy, Kate," he said. "And I think I'm falling for you. But if you don't get dressed, we'll never leave this tent."

Minutes later, dressed, she sat beside him.

"We need to focus," he said. "We're going in after Tara and I don't want to see any casualties, at least, not of anyone I care about."

Anyone I care about.

Those words seemed to hang between them, meaning so many things both spoken and not.

"I know you hate waiting," she said, trying to forget his words that had the power to change so much. "But I really don't think they have a clue what they're doing. I'm beginning to think, like we talked about last night, that we should wait until tonight. It will throw them off, which is better for us."

"If we at least get into position before nightfall, I can live with that." He stood. "Let's start getting this packed up so we're ready to move." He turned around. "And, for the record, I'd do it again," he said.

A slow smile spread across her face. "For the record—we will."

"Darn sure of yourself," he said as he leaned over to give her a chaste kiss on the cheek.

She twisted so that the kiss landed on her lips and she took it to the next level. The kiss was hot, open-mouthed, ripe with desire and the promise of more. But she pulled away as his body began demanding to take charge.

"I am very sure of myself," she replied. "Now, let's get your sister."

Chapter Eighteen

Wednesday, September 16th, 11:00 a.m.

"Let's do this," Kate said as she pulled out her gun, checked the chamber and holstered it. She turned to look at him with zeal for the assignment alive in her eyes. There was a confidence about her that was all about succeeding, and that confidence was contagious.

They'd spent the earlier part of the morning scouting the terrain backing into the oasis. There had been no sign of the last man who had shot at them, but they'd been prepared if he had showed up. When they got back to the tent there was nothing to show that it had been disturbed. No footprints, no evidence that anyone, other than them, had been there.

"Looks like our guess was right. I doubt if their sniper even knew what he was shooting at. He couldn't see much in the storm," Kate said. "They know someone's here. I don't think they had a visual, but sound travels. It's clear that they had a watch."

"I think you're right," Emir agreed.

"It's rough terrain. I doubt if we'll be able to make anywhere near the average 2.4 miles an hour. So…" She looked at her watch.

"We leave in an hour," he said as he pocketed the compass, loaded his Glock and stuffed two spare magazines into his pocket. He shifted his knapsack where she knew he had another couple of magazines, just as she did in hers. They were both prepared to hold off an army if necessary.

"Let's do it," Kate said less than an hour later.

"Kate," he said, taking her into his arms and kissing her hot, brief and full of promise.

They both knew this would be the only reference to what was growing between them. After, it would be all business.

And as if to confirm that, he let her go as quickly as he had pulled her against him. It was like they'd never been intimate. It was what they had to do, for they needed to be focused. One mistake could jeopardize everything and everyone.

For the moment it appeared they had the advantage. The kidnappers didn't know that she and Emir were out here. At least so they hoped, for just ten minutes ago Zafir had contacted them to let them know there had finally been another ransom demand, this time with specific instructions. They wanted a helicopter drop with an unarmed pilot at an oasis thirty miles to the south of the location where they now had them pinpointed. That wasn't going to happen. Now it was just a matter of getting Tara out.

Unfortunately, the kidnappers knew someone was here, it was only a matter of time before they put the pieces together.

"If we come in from the northwest corner, there's what I believe is a crevice that leads to a tunnel through a cave and goes straight through and into the oasis, hopefully near where they're holding her. I don't know how big it is, but I know the children, when the oasis was a settlement, used to use it," Kate said with an almost breathy excitement in her voice.

"How do you know this? You have no access to internet, no…"

"At the village. El Dewar. The women had more to say than what I told you." She shrugged. "An old lady I met was born here, in these very hills, on the oasis we're heading for."

"Anything else?"

"No one uses the oasis anymore, at least, not to live. In fact, she said it was mostly forgotten. Dried up when she was a child. She thought that there was some water, enough for a traveler or two. I'd say that makes it about perfect."

He smiled and put a hand on her shoulder. "Let's go."

The valley was narrow and surrounded by low-lying sandstone hills. The oasis was on the other side of the valley and, from what she had gleaned from the atlas, backed two steep hills at the end of the chain that served to protect it from outsiders.

"From what that woman said and what I've calculated," Kate said hours later, "we should be close to the break in the rock that would take us in." They'd been moving carefully through the valley throughout the afternoon. Now, the sun was setting and spilling a vibrant orange across the valley and up into the hills that stood like ancient sentinels, protecting the valley from intruders.

"We go up from here and through the rocks there," Kate said a few minutes later as she pointed to her right and about two hundred feet up.

They began to make their way up the narrow, steep path that wound between the rocks. Within twenty-five feet the path became smooth, almost worn, making it clear that at one time it had been a well-traveled route.

"The tunnel that leads into the oasis shouldn't be much farther," she said.

The rock rose on either side as high as Emir's shoulders, then the path narrowed and he found himself occasionally clipping his shoulders against outcroppings.

"They must have used this path to get water or maybe for defense. I believe they more frequently came in from the other way," Kate said. "From the oasis."

They both knew it was irrelevant what the path

had been used for. What mattered was that it was there and that they knew of its existence.

He was glad that she had been in El Dewar to listen to the musings of an old woman. Between that and the other women who had spoken to her, in the end, despite her unease, she'd succeeded. In an odd way, the women had trumped the men. He wondered what Tara would say about that and, at the thought of Tara, the old fury rolled in his gut. They were so close.

We're here, Tara, he said silently, as if his sister were privy to his thoughts.

"We'll get her out, Emir," Kate said. She stopped and took his hands in hers. "We'll get her out," she repeated and rose up on tiptoes to kiss him.

He took her in his arms and kissed her with all the emotion he was feeling. When he let her go, somehow he felt better, more centered and less angry.

That was something Kate did for him, among so many others. He felt like he'd known her forever and, as much as he wanted to find Tara, he dreaded the moment when he'd have to let Kate go. He pushed the thought out of his mind, for it was those kinds of thoughts that got one killed or worse, got one's partner killed. That would never happen. He wouldn't let it.

"Let's go," she said and they continued to make their way along the trail as it rose up and then began to go downward.

Finally they came to a dark hollow, a cave that Kate claimed the old woman had told her tunneled through the cliff and straight into the oasis. It was a long shot, but it was all they had. The light was scant as the penlight flickered off the rocky path. They had more powerful flashlights but this was all they could chance without risking the light might be seen.

"Cover me," he said. "And I'll go in."

"You won't fit," she replied.

"You don't know that." The opening was five feet high by four wide, plenty of room. He bent and entered the tunnel, but within seven feet it became drastically smaller. He shone the light ahead to see that the tunnel curved and realized that he would never get through. This tunnel was made for a smaller person. Reluctantly he backed out.

"We can go around…" he began.

"And let them know we're here. Ring the doorbell before entering—so to speak," she said and didn't tone down the sarcasm. "I'm sorry, that was uncalled for." She put a hand on his shoulder. "Let me, Emir."

"No…"

"Think of it, if the kidnappers are there, they're protected. If we come in from the oasis, we'd be in the open with no idea as to what their setup is. We'd be sitting ducks. No help to Tara. I can make it through the tunnel. At least, I can try," she whispered frantically. "I need to do this, Emir. We have no choice. You know that."

Reluctantly he nodded. "If she's not near, or if she is and you can't get her attention, come back. Any trouble at all...come back."

"Don't worry." She adjusted her holster, moving it to her back so she could more easily crawl on her belly if necessary.

She took the small penlight then gave him a kiss.

He pulled her against him, his lips ravishing hers, opening her mouth, bending her back as if the passion in the kiss would somehow protect her. When he let her go, they stood looking at each other as if it was the last time they'd get to do that. He pushed that thought from his mind. It wouldn't happen. She was too skilled, too smart, and he cared for her too much.

"Be careful."

"No worries," she said, her lips red from his kisses.

She turned and ducked into the tunnel. He shone his light on her until she disappeared and all he wanted to do was follow her.

He was left to wait. He couldn't leave his post. He had to remain there, waiting in case she might need him.

He paced.

THE TUNNEL NARROWED almost immediately and then opened up so that Kate was able to walk with her head down. The rock was cool and the passage narrow enough that her shoulders occasionally scraped rock. She could hear faint scratching and movement from somewhere within the tunnel and her flashlight caught sight of a black beetle that froze and then scurried away. She could see why children used this route, but a grown adult wouldn't as at one point she was doubled over and her knees were bent.

The low ceiling and the narrowness had her fighting feelings of claustrophobia and wrestling with the idea of retreating. A minute later she came around a turn and then another going right and then left. Suddenly she could hear male laughter and saw a flicker of light. She turned off the penlight.

The smell of cigarette smoke wafted around her and was intertwined with the smell of burning wood and of what she guessed might be the smoke from a campfire. She squatted, knowing she was near the exit, and waited. If she were able to smell the cigarette smoke over the fire, then the smoker wasn't far from her position. She waited, sniffing the air. Five minutes passed before she could smell nothing but the fire. Whoever the smoker had been, they'd either put it out or moved away. She had to take her chances and hope it was the latter.

She got down on her hands and knees and crawled the remaining distance as the tunnel twisted before she saw another flicker of light. There was a palm tree growing up against the rock, partially hiding the opening. She could see the snap of flames about fifty feet away and as she looked down there was a movement. But she couldn't make out anything in the dark. She squatted back on her heels. As she contemplated what to do next, the night sky cleared and the moon shone bright and revealing. She looked down and met the terrified eyes of Sheikka Tahriha Al-Nassar.

Kate put her fingers to her lips and the woman nodded while avidly watching her. She pointed at Tara and then back at the tunnel where she crouched so that it was clear what she wanted her to do and where she wanted her to go, once she managed to free her. It was a backup plan, nothing else. So that if anything happened to her, as long as she was untied, Tara could still get out and to safety.

Kate looked toward the campfire and saw that there were three men. She could hear their voices and laughter and, as the flames danced, she could also see that they were sitting with their backs to her. The tricky part would be getting Tara free, for they could see in the moonlight as easily as Kate could.

She slid down the path that wound steeply from the tunnel to the hill. She kept low and used her feet to control and steer her way while remaining hidden from the men by the shrubbery growing up against the hill.

With a bump she was on her butt on level ground and the only thing that stood between her and discovery was a grassy bush and another palm tree. She looked over and Tara was watching her. Kate shook her head and the woman looked away.

She could see that Tara's hands were tied behind her back and secured to the trunk of a palm tree. She could also see that they'd only used rope. They obviously hadn't expected much resistance and she hadn't expected that it would be that easy. She fished the knife she always carried out of her pocket. It couldn't be called a pocketknife but it couldn't be called a hunting knife, either. All she knew was that it could slide through any kind of rope with ease.

She held her breath, watching the men. They were caught up in their conversation, and none was paying attention. She'd be in the open for a minute, the time it took to get to Tara. She just needed Tara to back up against the palm tree. She waited until the woman glanced at her and she motioned to the tree. Tara moved until her back was pressed against it.

Smart, Kate thought. So far she was following every cue with ease.

Kate moved in swiftly, keeping low to the ground. Within a minute Tara was free and Kate had given her whispered directions and she was off.

Kate turned on her heels, moving to face the kidnappers; it only took a second but it was enough. As she went to follow Tara she was grabbed roughly from behind.

"What are you doing?" the male voice snarled in Arabic.

"Run!" she yelled at Tara and saw her scramble up the last few feet and disappear into the tunnel.

His grip on her arm was so tight Kate bit her lip against the pain as he twisted her around.

"Where's the sheikka? Where is she?" he roared, his face half hidden by a shaggy beard, his eyes wild, not focusing on her as his hand bit into her arm.

Her other arm was free and with it she quietly moved to reach her gun without drawing his attention to what she was doing.

But as he looked up toward the tunnel, he yanked her arm hard, ramming it up between her shoulders and making her bite back a shriek of pain, causing her other hand to drop from where she had been inching toward her weapon.

"Get her back! Get her now!" he shrieked into her face.

"Run, Tara!" Kate screamed and it was the last thing she did as her captor's fist connected with her jaw.

Chapter Nineteen

"Zafir, I've got her."

Emir gave his brother little time to express his relief or to explain the circumstances. The connection was tentative and could break at any moment. He looked over to where Tara was guzzling the contents of a water bottle. Other than being stressed and dehydrated, his baby sister was fine.

"They've got Kate," he said through clenched teeth. He would have gone in with guns blazing but that wouldn't have done Kate or Tara any good. "I need to go in after her but I need to get Tara out of here, to safety, first."

"Is it Ed?" Zafir asked in a strained voice.

"That's what Tara tells me," Emir said, holding anger back with an iron will as he gave Zafir the co-ordinates. "How soon can you get here?"

Zafir promised he'd be there soon with Talib, and that they were minutes away. Emir almost sighed. If he lost Kate now, before she knew how he felt about her… The thought trailed. She didn't know that those intimate moments were about more than just lust. It had all been too soon and too fast, and yet it had been like a lifetime. In such a short time, he felt like he'd always known her and, unbelievably, he'd fallen in love with her.

But none of that mattered. What mattered was that they had her, that she was in danger. The thought was killing him as much as the knowledge that there was nothing he could do. He couldn't leave Tara, for they would be looking for her soon, unless somehow they thought Kate was the trade-off. His thoughts were jumbled. He couldn't think clearly and he needed to get it together and get it together now. Kate as a trade-off was a thought he couldn't discard and one that made him every bit as sick as them having his sister.

"She came just in time," Tara whispered as he sat beside her. "He was crazed. Thought I was Mother." She shook her head. "I can't believe it was Ed. He wasn't who I remember. He would have raped me if he'd had much longer."

Or worse, Emir thought as rage rolled through him as he listened and he wanted to kill. He took a few breaths, stilling his emotions. He needed to get through this calmly. After all, Tara wasn't out of danger yet.

Where was Zafir? Emir had to go after Kate and in one crazy moment he considered taking Tara with him.

"Ridiculous," he muttered.

"Em. You're scaring me," Tara said.

Emir looked at his sister and guilt ran through him. She'd been through hell. "It'll be okay, kid. I promise," he said. "Zafir will be here any moment to get you out of here."

"You care for her, don't you," she said in a quiet voice. "Kate." She said the name as if testing it out. After all, Tara had only learned the name of her rescuer a few moments ago. "She'll make it, Em, she has to."

Has to. Tara's words echoed in their rightness, for he didn't know what he'd do if she didn't.

He took her hands in both of his. "He didn't hurt you? You're certain?" He had two reasons to kill the man now, he thought ferociously. Kate and Tara. It was odd, there were others, but to him it was Ed who had betrayed his family.

"No." She shook her head. "But I never knew... I can't believe... I mean, he loved Mother. He was crazy for her. I mean nutcase crazy. And it made me think about their accident. His face was burned..." She looked at Emir. "You don't think...?"

"Let's talk about that later," Emir said as he thought of the unspeakable act Ed had perpetrated on the House of Al-Nassar. He didn't need to bring down his family, he'd dealt them a crushing blow broadsiding the family, destroying its heart, and no one had known, until now.

Emir shuddered at the thought and again at the thought of what a nightmare this man must have been for his mother. No wonder the mention of letting him go had left her lips when usually she had left employment issues to his father. To think that his parents were dead, partially or wholly, because of this man—rage ran through him.

"I just wanted to go to a party, alone. To look normal, without security trailing me, and I ditched them." She burst into tears, her head in her hands.

"Tara, sweetheart." He put an arm awkwardly around her, his gun still in that hand, and aware of the importance of time. "It's all right. You're safe and this will never happen again."

"It won't," she mumbled. "I promise."

"Look at me," he said.

She looked up.

"We don't have much time. I need you to take a deep breath and think of where they held you. Tell me what their setup is."

"Emir, you're not…"

"Tell me." He chucked her under the chin with his free hand as he had when she'd been a child. In an odd way it made both of them feel better. "I won't let you down."

"You mean you won't let yourself get killed. Promise me, Emir."

"Promise."

And he listened as Tara explained what she knew

of the three heavily armed men who had kidnapped her and the remains of a forgotten oasis where she'd been held. And as he listened, the rage he had tamped down so effectively became like steel, cold and lethally determined.

It was minutes later when he heard the distant whir of a helicopter. He switched on the flashlight and waved it. The powerful light was unlike the minute one that Kate had used on the way into the cave. In fact, it was one used by top scientists working in the desert and threw a powerful beam of light.

Within minutes the helicopter was down and Tara was surrounded. It was only once Talib and Zafir had determined to their satisfaction that she wasn't physically injured that Tara was lifted into a bear hug from which Talib seemed determined not to release her.

"Let's get her out of here." Emir's voice brought everyone back to business. And within minutes Tara was in the helicopter and off with Talib while Zafir stayed behind.

"They've got Kate," Emir said, the anguish clear in his voice as he briefed his brother on all that Tara had told him.

"She's got your heart, man," Zafir said and there was a hint of surprise in his voice. He pulled the safety on his handgun and turned to his brother. "Let's get her."

They didn't have a choice other than to go in from

the front, but with the detail Tara had provided, they at least knew how to get close enough unobserved.

When they arrived they found the camp was like nothing Tara had described, instead it was chaos. The fire burned low and cans and empty bottles lay everywhere. In the center of the oasis were the remains of a tent, much of the canvas strewn around the area as if it had been destroyed in a fit of anger.

On the edges, where the desert met the oasis, they could hear the voices of at least two men. Angry but unclear as to what they were saying.

"We've got to locate Kate," Emir said.

Zafir nodded and together they made their way along the perimeter of the oasis.

Twenty feet in, Emir saw her as the moon and the waning fire provided some light. Kate's hands and feet were tied and her shirt was ripped partially off. Her hair was tangled and loose, but it was when he eased closer that he had to use all his willpower to keep silent. Her lip, jaw and cheek were swollen and blood trailed down her chin. He didn't dare go any closer without threatening their cover.

She looked up and, despite her state, smiled. Her eyes shifted to where the men argued. Their voices were getting louder and it was clear they were only focused on each other.

Emir looked back at Kate. She looked toward the men and closed her eyes twice, slowly, deliberately.

Then she did it again, this time once, and then she looked up and over the hill.

Emir gave her a single nod. He knew she was telling him that one of the men had already made his escape over the hill, possibly in search of Tara. That thought both enraged and frightened him. They needed to move fast.

He looked at Kate. Any sound could alert the men. He needed to free her, but getting any closer could be tricky. He pulled out his dagger and motioned for Zafir to stay back.

Emir moved in carefully, slipping behind her, using her as a shield to screen his presence. He sliced through the rope that bound her wrists—silently, quietly, desperately wanting to speak to her, to hold her—he could do neither.

There was a shout, garbled words, and he feared they'd been discovered.

"Give me the knife," she whispered urgently.

"Go through the tunnel," he said. "I'll meet you on the other side."

She nodded, taking the knife from him as a beam of light settled on her and a harsh voice in Arabic demanded to know what she was doing.

Emir moved behind the trunk of a palm tree. He could see the shadow of Zafir across from him. He motioned forward. They needed to get away from Kate—to get her out of the line of fire.

Emir picked up a rock, glanced at Zafir and threw

it, hitting one of the men in the arm. He swung around, cursing angrily in Arabic as the other man reached for the rifle slung over his back and the second pulled a handgun. Emir smiled. He didn't want to kill a man by blindsiding him. That wouldn't be fair, no matter what he'd done. He glanced back. Kate was gone.

Despite thoughts of giving them a chance, it was less than a minute before both men were dead.

"One shot," Zafir grumbled. "Too easy."

Emir went over, kicking the one man in the shoulder and pushing the body over. There was no sign of life. He did the same with the other. Neither was the man responsible for it all.

"Where's Ed?" He turned to look at Zafir and alarm raced in unspoken words between them.

"There's no sign of anyone else," Zafir said.

Emir didn't answer, he was on the run, going back—making sure that Kate, too, was gone—safe.

She was nowhere in sight, not at the base of the hills, not in the entrance of the tunnel.

There was no one else in the oasis.

Ten minutes later they were on the other side of the oasis where they'd started out. In the darkness they could see nothing.

"Son of a desert stray, where is she?" Emir growled, his heart pounding at the thought of Ed still on the loose and Kate nowhere to be found.

"We've got company," Zafir said. "Just behind us at ten o'clock."

He'd no sooner said that when a shot came from the hills and echoed through the rocks.

"Ed!" Emir shouted as a means of a diversion as Zafir moved into position to his left. "What are you doing, man? You were my father's friend."

"Damn Al-Nassar!" came the shout from what sounded like near the base of the hill. "You always had everything."

"Give yourself up, man," Emir ordered. He moved forward and to the right as Zafir continued to move in the opposite direction.

"It's not worth it!" Zafir shouted in a perfect imitation of Emir's voice.

Arabic curses followed. "Which one of you bloody look-alikes are you?"

Overhead, the rotors of a helicopter beat the air and overrode their voices.

"Son of a… Talib," Emir swore. Minus a brother, his whole family was here. He hoped Talib had the sense to keep Tara out of this, to have dropped her in a safe place before returning. He couldn't afford to think otherwise.

He moved forward in the darkness, using one boulder and then another for cover.

Where was she?

"Emir?" It was a whisper in the dark. A sound meant only for him, and close, too close.

"Kate," he said. His voice was soft, controlled, so it wouldn't carry. "Get back."

And then he saw her. He moved in beside her. There was no time for discussion. He'd take a hit for her if necessary. The thought, despite the intensity of the situation, startled him. He'd never felt like that about any woman. With the exception of his mother and his sister, there had been no woman he would have taken a bullet for. He felt that and more about Kate.

The light from the helicopter swept the area. It was blinding as bullets cut through the night and he crouched beside Kate behind a rock from where he could see Zafir slowly making his way around, cutting off any chance of escape, using the distraction of the helicopter to his advantage.

"Stay down," he said as he prepared to move in.

Kate nodded. There was nothing she could do. They'd taken her gun.

There was movement ahead and Emir could see the top of Ed's head as he sought better cover. He fired at him and Ed shot back, the bullet whining through the valley. Then there was a shot from the left, as Zafir joined the battle.

A series of shots followed.

"Ed," Emir called when a temporary silence descended. "Mother's been asking about you."

"You're lying," he snarled.

"Stay here," he said to Kate. "I'm going after him."

He moved forward, going from one rock to the next in the direction of the voice. The helicopter had pulled back and they were again in darkness.

"She misses you," Emir said as he moved another few feet forward.

"Why did she run away?"

The voice was just ahead and to his left. Something moved and suddenly he was there, facing the man he barely recognized and who had once been his father's shadow.

Emir didn't wait but instead launched himself at Ed, driving him down with an uppercut to the chin followed by another to the temple. Ed's gun clattered to the rocks as Emir hit him again. This time Ed stumbled and fell.

"Maybe next time you'll think twice about hitting women or destroying families," Emir snarled. But he knew that there wouldn't be a next time. Ed would die before this night was over.

Light bounced over the rock and he could see Kate using a boulder for cover and trying to give him some help as she shone the flashlight at Ed. He was glad of the help as he saw Ed had found his gun. But Emir fired before Ed could raise it into position. Ed tumbled backward, landing heavily in the rocks.

The helicopter had moved in again, preparing to land. The blades were creating a wind that emulated a sandstorm as it threatened to pull their clothes from their bodies.

"I can't believe it, Em," Zafir said minutes later as they stood a few feet from Ed's body. "This piece of camel's offal killed our parents."

"He was in love with our mother and, from what I've pieced together, thought he'd kill our father to have her. In the process he killed them both."

"He was unbalanced to begin with, but he lost all reason as a result," Kate added. "Eventually believing that your mother still lived."

"Son of a desert dog!" Zafir cursed. "I wish he'd lived just so I could have the pleasure of killing him."

"It's over, Zaf," Emir said and threw an arm over his shoulder. "We took him out. Tara's safe."

He let his brother go and moved over to Kate. His finger gently ran along her jaw. "I'm sorry he hurt you. I'd kill him again if it would prevent that."

"I'm okay, Emir, really." She took his face in her hands, pulled him gently toward her and kissed him.

"And the house of Al-Nassar stands to see another day," Talib said as he led the way to the helicopter. "Let's get out of here. Let the authorities clean up this stinking pile of offal."

"I can't believe Ed kidnapped Tara. I mean, I get that he in some crazed way thought she was Mother, who he was in love with," Zafir said as they walked to the helicopter. "But why the blackmail?"

"I can't believe any of this," Talib said. "I wish I'd been the one to kill him. He murdered our parents. And why come after us again six years later?"

Kate looked from one to the other and saw the pain reflected on all of their faces. "From what the police records indicate, your parents' accident was initially just that—an accident. It was what happened after that…" She hesitated, feeling Emir's pain, feeling all their pain. "That became murder."

"It's ugly, guys," Emir said thickly. "Basically when the car accident happened, Ed was there as he usually was to act as bodyguard. My first thought was that he murdered them, that he was responsible, but his last words to me admitted otherwise. And there's no way to prove it. Anyway, he said that he got out of the car and wouldn't let our father out. By the time he got around to trying to help Mother, who was trapped in the back, it was too late. The driver was trapped by the steering wheel. The resulting fire ignited an explosion, and you know the rest. Ed admitted that just before he tried to shoot me."

"Thank goodness you shot first," Kate said.

"Murdering pile of dung deserved a harder death," Talib said with clenched fists.

"You're right," Kate said. "He was a murderer, but he was also sick. I think the guilt of what he did ate at him. I'm not sure when he suffered the next psychotic break but eventually that led him to do what he did. The fact that it took six years." She shrugged. "Hard to predict a broken mind."

She put an arm around Emir's waist and smiled reassuringly at him.

"He thought he could live with Tara, who he saw as Mother, in the lifestyle to which he knew she enjoyed. That's why he needed the money," Emir said. "He was as twisted and broken as his kidnapping plot, and the others were just along for the ride and the money."

"Definitely twisted," Zafir agreed. "And the airport attackers were small-time crooks hired by Ed. They decided it might be easier to get their cash if they took you out, Em. I don't think that was part of Ed's plan."

"Unbelievable," Emir said with a shake of his head. "Ed couldn't keep control of the scum he hired."

"That's why the woman from El Dewar remembered Ed, not just because of your name, but because he'd recently been there hiring help to take us out. Seems every place has their lowlife," Kate said, remembering the shady man in El Dewar who had looked at her oddly and the bikers that had tried to gun them down, so soon after, in the desert.

Emir shrugged. "That pretty much sums it up."

A HALF HOUR later they were settled in the helicopter and, with Zafir piloting, they began to lift off.

"It was a horrible thing—your parents' accident, Tara's kidnapping. I can't imagine what Tara went through. At least it's finally over." She looked at Emir and her heart beat just a little harder, and despite everything that had happened, she didn't want to leave and return to Wyoming. Not yet. Not without Emir at her side. She pushed back those thoughts. They were ridiculous, her life was there—his was here.

"Is it?" Emir asked. "There's one piece of this whole ugly mess that I'm not so sure I want to be over." His hand ran gently over her rapidly bruising jaw as his eyes met hers, and it was clear that it wasn't Tara's kidnapping he was talking about but the feelings that had grown between them. And despite the time and place—it seemed right, for everything they felt had begun in the heat of this crisis.

"What are you saying?" she asked.

His arm went around her shoulders in an oddly familiar way, as if they'd known each other for a very long time.

"What would you think of spending some time in Marrakech?"

"On assignment?"

"Sightseeing. I think you've earned a vacation," he said as he turned her to face him. His intense eyes met hers and his full lips were… She couldn't look away as he leaned over to claim her lips, his arms bringing her hard and fast against him. "I want you here where I can always see you, where I will never let you go."

"Emir…"

"Later. For now let's just say that I may love you."

"Oh, for the love of Allah, Em. Tell the woman straight up."

"Could we have a moment, Zaf?" Emir said. He turned to Kate and whispered in her ear, "I love you."

And as he bent to kiss her, she met the kiss with all the passion in her heart. "Given some time, I may feel the same," she said, but her heart pounded and seemed to tell her that time wouldn't change anything. She loved him now.

"Then that's all we need," he said as he pulled her tighter against him.

And in the towns and villages of Morocco as he kissed her one more time, the call to prayer was beginning as if the entire country approved of a love that was definitely in the air.

* * * * *

Look for more books in Ryshia Kennie's
DESERT JUSTICE *in 2017.*
You'll find them wherever
Harlequin Intrigue books are sold!

THE SCENE WAS all wrong.

The killer—the balding man in his late thirties—the man who stood there with sweat dripping down his face, a gun held in his trembling hand and a dead girl at his feet...he was *wrong*.

FBI Special Agent Samantha Dark raised her weapon even as she shook her head. She'd profiled this killer, studied every detail of his crime spree. And...

This is wrong.

"Drop the gun!" That bellow came from her partner, Blake Gamble. He was at her side, his weapon drawn, too, and she knew all of his focus was locked on the killer.

They'd come to this house just to ask Allan March some follow-up questions. He'd been one of the custodians at Georgetown University, a university that had recently become the hunting grounds for a killer.

At Blake's shout, Allan jerked. And when he jerked, his finger squeezed the trigger of the gun he held. The shot went wide, missing both Samantha and Blake. She didn't return fire. *Allan doesn't fit the profile. This is all wrong—*

Blake returned fire. The bullet slammed into Allan's right shoulder. Not a killing wound, not even close. Blood bloomed from the spot, soaking the stark white shirt that Allan wore. Allan should have dropped his gun in response to that hit, but he didn't. He screamed. Tears trickled down his cheeks, and he aimed that gun—

Not at Blake, but at me.

"Has to be you…" Allan whispered. "Said…*has to be you…*"

She didn't let any fear show, even as the emotion nearly suffocated her. "Allan, put down the gun." Blake's order had been bellowed, but hers was given softly. Almost sadly. *Put the gun down, Allan. I don't want to shoot you. This isn't the way I want things to end.*

The FBI had been searching for the Georgetown University killer for months. Following the trail left by the bastard—a trail of blood and bodies. But the trail shouldn't have led here.

Allan March was a widower. His wife had passed away two years ago, slowly dying of cancer. He'd been at her bedside every single moment. All of the data that the FBI had collected on Allan indicated that he was a dedicated family man, a caregiver. Not—

A serial killer.

"I'm sorry," Allan whispered.

And Samantha knew what he was going to do. Even as those tears poured down his cheeks, she *knew*.

"No!" Samantha screamed.

But it was too late. Allan pointed the gun right at his own face and pulled the trigger. The thunder of the gunfire echoed around them, and, a moment later, Allan's body hit the floor, falling to land right next to the dead body of Amber Lyle, the twenty-two-year-old college student who'd been missing for three days.

"Fucking hell," Blake muttered.

This is wrong.

Samantha rushed toward the downed man. Her weapon was still in her hand. Her eyes were on Allan. On what was left of his face. *Dear God.*

"THE PRESS IS ripping us apart, Samantha! Ripping us apart!" Her boss glared at her as they stood inside the small FBI office. "You were supposed to be the freaking superstar—a profiler who could do no wrong. But your profile was *shit*. You had us looking for a man who didn't exist. Three women died while we were looking for the killer *you* said was out there!"

Samantha stood, her shoulders back and her spine straight, as Justin Bass berated her. Spittle was flying from her boss's mouth. His blue gaze blazed with rage.

The executive assistant director was far more pissed than she'd ever seen him before. The guy had a temper, everyone knew that truth, but this time... *There's no going back.*

Justin didn't like to look bad. He liked to be the agent in charge, the man with the answers. The suit who handled the press and gloried in the attention he got when his team brought down the bad guy.

"Damn it, Samantha!" Justin snarled, a muscle twitching in his rounded jaw. "Do you have anything to say?"

Did she? Samantha swallowed. Did she dare tell him what she thought? When every single piece of evidence said just how wrong she'd been?

"Take it easy, Bass." Blake spoke on her behalf. He was at her side, sending her a sympathetic glance. "What matters is that the Sorority Slasher has been stopped."

The Sorority Slasher. Samantha hated that name. It sounded like something from a really bad horror flick. Leave it to the tabloids to glam up a grisly killer.

"We're the fucking FBI," Justin said, stopping to slap his hands down on his desk. "We can't afford to make mistakes."

Her temples were throbbing. She knew exactly who they were.

"Someone has to take the fall for this one. *Three* women died because you were wrong. *You* were wrong, Samantha. The superstar from Princeton. The woman who was supposed to change the face of profiling. FBI brass shoved you down my throat, and you were *wrong*."

She made her jaw unclench.

"You're taking the fall for this one." Justin nodded curtly toward her. "Consider yourself on suspension."

Samantha almost took a step back. Her lips parted—

Don't take the job from me.

"What?" Blake was the one who'd given that shocked cry. It was Blake who sounded furious as he snapped, "You can't do that! Samantha is the best—"

"Yeah, right, you think I don't know about the hard-on you have for her, Agent Gamble?" Justin fired right back. "You two *never* should have been partners. So take some advice, buddy. Save your own ass. She's a sinking ship, and you don't want to go down with her."

Her boss was a bastard. Lots of men she'd met in the FBI were arrogant assholes. Blake? No, he was a good guy, and that was why she respected him so much.

"Leave your weapon here," Justin ordered her. "And your badge."

She unsnapped her holster, walked slowly toward his desk.

My profile was right. I know it was.

She put her gun on his desk, but when she reached for her FBI badge and ID, Samantha hesitated.

"You know, we found pictures of all the victims at his place." Justin's voice was flat. "Souvenirs that he kept."

"Trophies." It was the first thing she'd said since coming into his office. "Not souvenirs, they're trophies." Serial killers often kept them so that they could relive their crimes.

"Shoved in the back of his closet, under the guy's winter boots." Justin shook his head. "Dropped like they didn't matter, and you spent all that time telling us we were looking for a cold, methodical killer. One who wanted to push boundaries and study the pain of his victims. One who wanted to see just how well matched he'd be with authorities. A smart killer, a damn genius. Fuck me, Samantha, Allan March barely graduated high school!"

And that was just one of the many reasons why he was *wrong*.

Her fingers had clenched around her ID. "Did you ever think…" Her voice was too soft, but it was either speak softly or scream. "Did you consider that maybe Allan had been set up?"

Justin's hands flew up into the air in a gesture of obvious frustration. "He shot himself! *Killed* his damn fool self when he blew off half his head! If that doesn't say guilty, then what the hell does?"

Her drumming heartbeat was too loud. "He could have killed himself for a number of reasons." Reasons that were nagging at her. He'd lost his life savings battling his wife's cancer. Extreme financial hardship? Hell, yes, that could lead people to suicide. It could—

Justin yanked the ID from her hand. "Get the hell out, Samantha. You are done. I won't have you talking this shit in my office—and you sure as hell better not plan on stopping to talk to the reporters outside."

"Director Bass—" Blake began angrily.

"Don't!" Justin threw right back at him. "Not another word, unless you want to be giving up your badge, too."

No, Blake wouldn't do that. The FBI was his life.

She kept her spine ramrod straight as she walked out of the office. When she reached the bull pen, she heard the whispers—from the other FBI agents there, from the cops who'd come to team up with them. Everyone was staring at her with confusion in their eyes.

She was wrong. She screwed up. She let those women die.

This was all going to be on her. Samantha clenched her hands into fists.

She made it to the elevator. One step at a time. Her spine was starting to hurt.

She slipped into the elevator. Pushed the button

to go down to the parking garage. The doors were starting to close—

"Samantha." Blake was there. Shoving his hand through the gap between the doors, trying to get to her.

She shook her head. "No." Because she couldn't deal with him right then. He pulled at her emotions, and she already felt too raw.

Blake. Handsome, strong Blake. Blake with his rugged good looks, his jet-black hair, his bright green eyes and that golden skin...sexy Blake.

Fierce Blake.

Off-limits Blake.

Because her bastard of a boss had been right about one thing. Blake did have a hard-on for her. She'd noticed his attraction. It would have been impossible to miss. An attraction that she more than felt, too. But he was her partner. You didn't screw around with your partner. That was against the rules.

She'd always played by the rules.

And she'd still gotten screwed.

"This isn't on you," Blake gritted out.

Actually, it was. The dead man's blood was still on her clothes because she'd run to him after he'd blown off half his face. His blood was on her—and the deaths of those three women? She knew her boss was going to push those her way, too. Before he was done, she'd be some rogue FBI agent who'd gone off the playbook—and he'd be the shining superstar who'd somehow managed to stop the Sorority Slasher.

Blake stepped into the elevator. Ignoring her request. The doors closed behind him, and his hands curled around her shoulders. "The profile was off. You're not God. You can't predict everything."

"I don't want you touching me." Her words came out stark and hard. Not at all the way she normally spoke to Blake.

He blinked, and, for an instant, she could have sworn that he looked hurt.

"Let me go." She didn't have time to choose her words carefully. She was about to break apart, and his touch was sending her closer and closer to the edge.

His hands fell away from her. He stepped back.

"I'm not dragging you down with me." She licked her lips. "You still have a chance here. You just had the bad luck to get teamed up with me."

"I don't think it's bad."

"Trust me, it is." Her heart was racing far too fast in her chest. "Just walk away." What had Bass called her? A sinking ship?

The elevator dinged. Finally, she was at the parking garage. Maybe she'd be able to get out of there without the reporters catching her. She stepped toward the elevator's now open doors, but Blake moved into her path.

Her head tipped back as she stared up at him.

"I want to help," Blake said.

There he went being the good guy. "Then let me go."

"Sam..."

"I'll call you tomorrow, okay?" She wouldn't, but, right then, she would have said anything to get away from him. Blake pushed her buttons. She'd always suspected he would have made for an amazing lover—and with her control being as shaky as it was at that particular moment, Samantha was afraid she would cross a line with him if she didn't get out of there.

Once you cross some lines, there is no going back...

A muscle flexed in Blake's square jaw, his green eyes gleamed, but he got out of her way.

She rushed past him. Nearly ran—and she didn't stop, not until she reached her car.

WHEN IT CAME to drinking, Samantha had always had an extremely high tolerance for alcohol. That had come, she suspected, courtesy of her dad. A tough ex-cop, he'd been able to drink anyone under the table.

So she sat in that low-end bar, on the wrong side of DC, and she studied the row of shot glasses in front of her.

"I knew I'd find you here. You always come to this place when you want to vanish."

She looked up at that deep, rumbling voice. A voice she knew—intimately, unfortunately. *Another line that I crossed a long time ago.* And her gaze met the dark stare of Cameron Latham. *Dr.* Cameron Latham. They'd known each other since their first year at university. Been friends, competitors. They'd gone all through college and graduate school together, earning their PhDs in psychology.

But after graduation, she'd joined the FBI. Samantha had wanted to use her talents to bring down criminals. And Cameron—he'd been bound for the Ivy League and a cushy college teaching job.

And for the college girls whom she knew he seduced. The guy had model good looks, so the women had always flocked to him. Now he had money and power to go with those looks. He'd finally gotten everything he wanted.

He has what he wants, and I just lost what I valued most. Talk about a totally shitty night.

"Guessing the story made the news?" Samantha muttered. This wasn't the kind of bar that had TVs. This was a dark hole made for drinking.

And vanishing.

"It made the news." He pulled out a chair, flipped it around and straddled the seat. "*You* made the news." He whistled. "That asshole of a boss really threw you under the bus."

She lifted another shot glass and drained it in a gulp.

"Drinking yourself into oblivion isn't going to make the situation better..." Cameron cocked his head and studied her.

Her brows shot up at that. "Cam, I'm not even close to oblivion."

He should know better.

"The case is wrong." She slammed down the glass. "Allan March is *wrong*. I don't buy it. The scene was too pat. He was too desperate. That guy isn't the one I was after."

Cameron blinked. "The reporter said plenty of evidence was on hand—"

"Like people don't get framed?" She laughed, and the sound was bitter. "I know all about that. My dad lost his badge because he got pulled into that BS about setting up drug dealers on his beat." Though her dad had always sworn he hadn't been involved in the frame-ups, his protests did little good for his reputation. "People get framed. It's a sad fact of the world." She pushed a glass toward Cameron.

He didn't take it. He never drank much, and when he did drink, it was only the best. Expensive wines and champagnes. Jeez, the guy loved his champagne. When they'd gotten their master's degrees, she remembered the way he'd gone out and bought that fancy bottle of—

"Why would someone want to frame that guy?" His quiet question jerked her from the memory of their past.

She rolled her shoulders. "Because Allan was con-venient." *Duh.* Wait, *duh*? Maybe she did need to slow down on the drinks. "An easy target. The custo-dian who kept to himself. The widower with no close friends. Maybe the perp I'm after wanted the atten-tion off his back, so he tossed Allan into the mix."

Cameron frowned. "Allan…he killed himself."

"That's the part I haven't worked out yet." But she would. "I don't understand that bit. I swear, I actually thought the guy was going to shoot *me*, but then he turned the gun on himself. Weird as hell." She reached for another shot glass. The bartender had done such a lovely job of lining them up for her. "Maybe he had a deal with the killer. I mean, Allan had a daughter, after all. One that needs money for college, money for life. And Allan didn't have any money. He barely had anything at all. Maybe the killer offered Allan money to take the fall. Maybe he was supposed to go out in a blaze of glory." Her eyes narrowed as she considered this new angle. If Allan had gotten a payoff, then perhaps she could find the paper trail. *Follow the money.* "But… Allan was a caretaker." Her voice dropped as Allan's pro-file spun in her head. "His nature was protective, so in the end, he *couldn't* shoot me. Couldn't shoot at Blake. That wasn't who he was." Her lashes lifted as realization hit her. "He couldn't attack us because *Allan March wasn't a killer.* Instead of shooting us, he turned the gun on himself. The only person he hurt was himself." Excitement had her heart racing.

But Cameron just shook his head. His hair—blond and perfectly styled, as always—gleamed for a moment when he leaned forward beneath the faint light over her table. "Normally, you know I love it when you bounce your ideas off me…"

Her temples were throbbing.

"But the man had a dead woman at his feet. That part made the news, too."

"And no blood on him," she mumbled. Because *that* had been bothering her. *That* was why the scene had been wrong. When they'd first arrived, Allan had been sweating in his white shirt—and there had been no blood on the shirt. *Not until Blake shot him.* "The vic's throat was slit—ear to ear—and Allan didn't have a drop of blood on him. He *should've* had her blood on him." She pushed to her feet. "I have to make Justin listen to me. I'm not wrong. Allan was just a fall guy. The real killer—"

Cameron surged to his feet. His hand wrapped around her arm. "You can't go to your FBI boss with alcohol on your breath and a wild theory spilling from your lips." His voice was grim. "You want more than a suspension? You want to lose the job forever?"

"I want to stop the killer!"

Don't miss
AFTER THE DARK by Cynthia Eden,
available April 2017 wherever
HQN Books and ebooks are sold.

www.Harlequin.com

COMING NEXT MONTH FROM

⊞ HARLEQUIN®

I N T R I G U E

Available April 18, 2017

#1707 LUCAS
The Lawmen of Silver Creek Ranch • by Delores Fossen
Texas Ranger Lucas Ryland knows his ex, Hailey Darrow, would only come to him if she had no other choice. And this time, she and their newborn son are both in danger.

#1708 QUICK-DRAW COWBOY
The Kavanaughs • by Joanna Wayne
All Dani Boatman wants is to manage her bakery and look after her beloved orphaned niece, Constance. But when someone threatens to take Constance away, it's cowboy Riley Lawrence who rides to the rescue.

#1709 NECESSARY ACTION
The Precinct: Bachelors in Blue • by Julie Miller
Detective Tom "Duff" Watson and Melanie Fiske both want justice, and his investigation into an arms-smuggling ring in the Ozarks may be the key to solving her father's murder. Can they succeed with the secrets held between them—and the desire?

#1710 ALPHA BRAVO SEAL
Red, White and Built • by Carol Ericson
After Navy SEAL Slade Gallagher saves her from Somali pirates, documentary filmmaker Nicole Hastings thinks the threat is over. But when terrorists follow her to New York City, the SEAL answers the call to duty.

#1711 FIREWOLF
Apache Protectors: Tribal Thunder • by Jenna Kernan
Filmmaker Meadow Wrangler would have burned alive if not for Apache hotshot Dylan Tehuano. When he comes under fire for arson and manslaughter, Dylan and Meadow will have to work together to stay ahead of the heat.

#1712 SHEIK'S RESCUE
Desert Justice • by Ryshia Kennie
Zafir Al-Nassar isn't only the joint head of Nassar Security, he's a flirt and a tease. With a Moroccan royal's life on the line, agent Jade Van Everett is determined to prove herself even as the tension between her and Zafir takes a turn toward seduction.

YOU CAN FIND MORE INFORMATION ON UPCOMING HARLEQUIN® TITLES, FREE EXCERPTS AND MORE AT WWW.HARLEQUIN.COM.

HICNM0417

"Don't make me draw my gun," he warned, and took hold
of her wrist in case she was about to try to get out the
door.

But she didn't try to escape.

A hoarse sob tore from her mouth, and Hailey eased
away from him. Just in case she had another weapon back
there, Lucas leaned over the seat and did a quick check
around her. He frisked her, too. Since she was wearing a
pair of loose green scrubs, a thin sweater and flip-flops,
there weren't many places she could conceal a weapon.

Still, after what'd happened three months ago, Lucas
looked.

His hand brushed against the side of her breast, and
she made a soft sound. Not the groan she'd made earlier.
This one caused him to feel that tug deep within his body.
But Lucas told that tug to take a hike.

Their gazes connected. Not for long. Lucas finished
the search and found nothing.

"Now keep talking," he insisted. "Tell me what happened to you. Why did you go on the run, and why didn't you tell anyone before now that you were out of the coma?"

She opened her mouth and got that deer-in-the-headlights look. What she didn't do was answer him.

"Enough of this," he mumbled.

He took out his phone to call Mason and then the sheriff, but as he'd done with her earlier, Hailey took hold of his hand. "Please don't tell your cousins. Not yet."

Since most of his Ryland cousins were cops, that wasn't what he wanted to hear. "Did you break the law? Is that why you were on the run?"

"No." She closed her eyes and shook her head. Her head wasn't the only thing shaking, though. She started to shiver, the cold and maybe the fear finally getting to her. "But I'm in trouble. God, Lucas, I'm in so much trouble."

He was about to curse at her for stating the obvious, but something else went through her eyes.

Fear.

"It won't take long for word to get out that I'm awake," Hailey said, speaking barely louder than a whisper. "And he'll find out."

"He?" Lucas snapped.

Hailey's voice cracked. "There's a killer after me."

Don't miss
LUCAS by Delores Fossen,
available May 2017 wherever
Harlequin® Intrigue books and ebooks are sold.

HIEXP0417

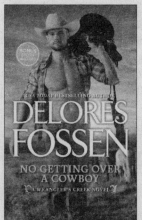